THE MAN WHO FOUND HIMSELF

Henri Duvernois

THE MAN WHO FOUND HIMSELF

Translated and introduced by
Brian Stableford

A Black Coat Press Book

Introduction

Henri Duvernois was one of those writers who was very popular in his day, when he was extremely prolific, but faded from memory somewhat thereafter, having owed his popularity primarily to his magnificent contemporaneity. He was famous as a short story writer, novelist and playwright—mostly of one-act comedies—but also produced numerous film-scripts, the occasional operetta, adaptations of Grimm's fairy tales and Daniel Defoe's *Robinson Crusoe* for children, biographies of Beethoven and the actor Victorien Sardou, and volumes of reflective memoirs. He once entered into a calculatedly-heterogeneous collaboration with Paul Bourget, Gerard d'Houville (Marie de Heredia, the wife of Henri de Régnier) and Pierre Benoît to produce the patchwork *Le Roman de quatre* (1923), and probably had more in common with each of his collaborators than any other two of them had with one another. He was honored in his lifetime with such prestigious awards as the Académie Française *Grand Prix de Littérature* (1933) and was appointed a *Commandeur de la Légion d'honneur*, but his name is nowadays most commonly encountered in the annals of the cinema, for which he did a good deal of writing in his later years, as well as supplying the bases for several notable film versions of his novels. The best-known of these films is perhaps the 1958 version of *Maxime* (1927), starring Charles Boyer.

The author's real name was Henri-Simon Schwabacher, and he was born in Paris on March 4, 1875 to a Hungarian father, who worked in the city as a diamond merchant, and a Dutch mother. He left school at 17 to go to work for the publisher Charpentier, in a clerical job, but he was already writing plays—*Le Troisième Larron* [The Third Larron], signed with his real name, was produced at the Cercle Pigalle on December 14, 1893—and that was always his true vocation. He soon embarked on supplementary adventures in journalism, contributing articles to various newspapers and magazines, including *Le Journal, Le Matin* and the humorous periodical *Comoedia*. He claimed that it was on the advice of Catulle Mendès that he first turned his hand to fiction, and he became a prolific contributor of short fiction to an ever-expanding range of periodicals before branching out into novels in the first decade of the new century, beginning with *Le Roseau de fer* [The Iron Reed] (1908).

In 1910, Duvernois married a German circus-rider and actress, who used the stage name Rita del Erido, although her real name was Margaretha Liebmann. This ascendant phase of his career was, however, interrupted—like so many other careers—by the Great War. He was unfortunate, or perhaps fortunate, in being wounded shortly after being recruited to active service in 1914; he spent the remainder of the war in pain, but mostly out of danger. While in hospital, he made the acquaintance of Guillaume Apollinaire, with whom he maintained a correspondence until the latter writer's premature death, and was briefly claimed for the cause of surrealism—André Breton was greatly impressed by his first post-war novel, *Edgar* (1919)—but he reverted to the light-heartedly cynical sophistication of his earlier plays and novels when he stepped up his production once again to its former extravagant scale.

In the 1920s, which became his heyday, Duvernois assisted the actor/playwright Sacha Guitry and the publisher Arthème Fayard in the foundation of the literary periodical *Oeuvres Libres*, to which he became a regular contributor of *romans* and *nouvelles*, wrote numerous theatrical comedies that enjoyed great success—many of which were vehicles for the actress Gaby Morlay—and wrote novels and scripts for silent movies in great profusion. He bought a villa in Antibes—the Villa Marguerite—at which many writers, actors and painters came to stay. He was greatly respected, as well as highly popular, as one of the principal chroniclers of and commentators on the decade that became known as the "roaring twenties" or the "Jazz Age" in America, but which Duvernois tended to refer to as the "années folles" [crazy years]. He continued to write prolifically in the early 1930s, but his health deteriorated gradually, and he died relatively young, 22 years before his wife, on January 30, 1937. He was buried in the Père Lachaise cemetery, a few plots along from Oscar Wilde.

Although he left behind a considerable number of unpublished works, which continued to appear posthumously until 1964, the last novel Duvernois published during his lifetime, which was probably the last one he completed, was *L'Homme qui s'est retrouvé* (1936), his only fantasy, here translated as *The Man Who Found Himself*. In terms of the literary device that activates its plot—a secretly-built starship that transports the protagonist to a planet orbiting Proxima Centauri—it qualifies a scientific romance, but it is a carefully and defiantly ambiguous narrative, which toys more dexterously than many other works that indulge in similar apologetic obfuscation with the possibility that the spaceflight might be a hallucinatory fantasy. As one of the earliest French texts to feature interstellar travel it has to be reckoned to have some significance in the history of French scientific romance, but the use of the motif is so manifestly artificial that its importance arguably has more to do with the rationalistic attitude it takes to a wholly fantastic situation than any vestige of technological plausibility.

Although the machine transporting the protagonist is deliberately characterized as a spaceship, and the world to which he is removed—after a journey of more than three years at the speed of light—is carefully identified as another planet, the journey he undertakes is essentially a trip in time rather than space. The other planet turns out to be identical to ours in every respect save one: its history is unfolding 40 years in arrears. His arrival there thus offers the protagonist the opportunity of "finding himself" in his late adolescence—an attractive prospect, because it offers an opportunity for him to avert the terrible misfortunes that are about to overwhelm his unwitting family.

The notion of other worlds recapitulating Earthly history was by no means new, but most previous instances had been scrupulously approximate, and had usually involved much more considerable lag phases, so Duvernois' version has more in common with such time-slip fantasies as Albert Robida's *L'Horloge des siècles* (1902; tr. in a Black Coat Press edition as *The Clock of the Centuries*) than with such time-lapsed duplication fantasies as Ellsworth Douglass's *Pharaoh's Broker* (1899), and perhaps even more with classic supernatural fantasies on the theme of the *doppelganger*. Like English, French has no exact equivalent of that German term, nor of the proverb that translates loosely into English as "he who sees his going double must go himself," but French writers and readers were sufficiently familiar with the German literary tradition to carry over some of the implications of that nest of ideas into fantasies about *doubles*, and there is some significance of that kind in

the fact that the protagonist of Duvernois' novel conti-
nually refers to his younger self as his *double* (which I,
of course, have translated as "double").

In view of this, it is probably safer to consider
L'Homme qui s'est retrouvé as a work of supernatural
fiction rather than a scientific romance, and to set it
squarely within the tradition of hallucinatory fantasy, but
Duvernois obviously had his reasons for invoking a
spaceship rather than a time machine or an explicit re-
presentation of a lunatic vision. Equally obviously, that
reason was the classic Wellsian motive of using a scien-
cefictional device and its attendant imaginative substance to add narrative muscle and tension to a classical
conte philosophique—as Voltaire, the great pioneer of
the *conte philosophique*, had done once himself in *Mi-
cromégas* (1735), thus founding the tradition of French
scientific romance. Yes, *L'Homme qui s'est retrouvé* is a
fantasy, which only really makes sense if it is construed
as a madman's manuscript, but it is a madman's manuscript that has substance and weight, which demands and
deserves serious pensive consideration even though—or
perhaps because—it is, at the end of the day, a literary
realization of a familiar daydream.

There is no way of knowing for sure, because there
are no secrets that people cling to more stubbornly than
the substance of their daydreams, but the private fantasy
of being able to go back in time within one's own life to
correct mistakes revealed in retrospect or explore forsa-
ken possibilities is probably extremely common, especially among people who have got to a point in life when
they feel, correctly or not, that they have run out of future. Even men like Henri Duvernois, who enjoy a glit-
tering career and every possible success, in addition to
sustaining lingering war-wounds, must be prone to this

kind of reflection—and how much more prone those people must be who feel that they have largely wasted their lives, having made horrible and fatal errors.

Given the probable near-universality of such regretful retrospection, it might be reckoned odd that there are not more literary developments of the theme, but the text of *L'Homme qui s'est retrouvé* takes the trouble to include an explanation of its own rarity, when the protagonist attempts to explain to his mother what has happened to him, by representing it as a dream. She comments, wisely, that such dreams always fall apart because they always collide eventually with some kind of contradiction, and cannot sustain their peculiar illogic in the ensuing battle of ideas. Actual dreams almost never deliver good raw material for literary work, except in the form of fugitive images that need to be carefully relocated in entirely different and more rational frameworks, and daydreams are only slightly better, even if one sets aside the problem of secrecy.

As conscious creations, daydreams are not as arbitrary in their combinations as dreams produced in sleep, but the vast majority of their tissues of wish-fulfillment are presumably (again I must speak in terms of probability, by virtue of the inevitable absence of statistical data) far too delicate to stand much contact with the calculus of rational extrapolation. As the substance of dreams must be recontextualized for literary re-examination, so must the substance of daydreams, and the resultant transplantation not only changes the literary result profoundly, but risks devastating the source-material, perhaps rendering it permanently unusable for private purposes thereafter. That kind of literary work is probably best avoided, except perhaps by men who think, or know, that they are about to die, and firmly believe that they will not need to fuel their daydreams for much longer.

Inevitably, the real subject of any literary work that enables a character to confront his past self is the struggle of contingency against destiny; equally inevitably, given what Omar Khayyam observed about the ineffectuality of our piety and wit to drag the moving finger back, contingency always starts out as the underdog. If a writer is careful to distance himself as much and humanly possible from his protagonist—as Charles Dickens from Scrooge, for example, when he rudely confronted the latter with his past, present and future selves—then he has the opportunity of writing a moral fable in which a measure of personal reorientation is possible, but the closer to home the fantasy strikes, the more an awareness of personal inelasticity is bound to take effect. In the most intense and intimate literary timeslip fantasies, which send protagonists back into the prison of their own early consciousness—the cardinal examples are P. D. Ouspensky's *Kinemadrama* (1915; tr. as *The Strange Life of Ivan Osokin*) and Louis Marlow's *The Devil in Crystal* (1944)—the effect can be spectacularly claustrophobic, and even trivial works of popular fiction that set out to use the motif as a mere gimmick sometimes entangle their authors more intricately than they intended. Thus, for instance, Robert A. Heinlein became so dissatisfied with the frothily ingenious "By His Bootstraps" (1941) that he eventually felt compelled to supplement it with the ruthlessly perverse egomaniac fantasy "All You Zombies..." (1957).

The most common title applied to fantasies more precisely aligned with Duvernois' version is "The Man Who Met Himself," most famously employed on a short film premièred at Cannes in 2005 but earlier employed

11

on the English version of a play by Luigi Antonelli (*L'Uomo che incontro se stesso*, 1918) and short stories by Donovan Bayley (1919), Ralph Milne Farley (1935), Eliot Crawshay-Williams (1947) and Edith Pargeter (1958). Duvernois might well have encountered a version of Antonelli's play, or the English play that probably inspired it, J. M. Barrie's *Dear Brutus* (1917), but he almost certainly drew the inspiration for his own story from an episode that made sufficient impact on him to prompt him to write an autobiographical essay, "Souvenirs," which he published in *Oeuvres Libres* 105 (1930), in which he describes a visit he paid to the house in which he and his parents had lived 40 years earlier, and the vivid memories that it awoke. Several other places mentioned in that reflective essay also crop up in *L'Homme qui s'est retrouvé*, and the novel also contains (quite gratuitously) an echo of the description in "Souvenirs" of a nostalgic visit Duvernois that paid to one of his old teachers. The fact that Duvernois chose a title with a slightly different significance from its more familiar counterpart is telling; his protagonist does simply *meet* an earlier version of himself, but by virtue of that encounter he *finds* himself, in the sense that he is able to reappraise and re-evaluate himself, not merely as he was but as he is—a realization in which destiny is bound to seem ineluctable, and from which little comfort is likely to be derivable.

Although *L'Homme qui s'est retrouvé* is obviously not autobiographical in any simple sense—its protagonist has followed a career trajectory very different from the author's—there is no doubt that the author felt easily able to identify with his creation, to whom he attributes a birth-date less than a year after his own. The timeslipped narrative is written almost entirely in the present tense, even though that makes little sense in the context of its supposed documentary nature, in order to maximize the sense of immediacy with which author and reader alike are able to share the fictitious experience. (Duvernois was acquainted with Parisian Existentialists as well as Surrealists, and he deserves some credit as a pioneer of stream-of-consciousness narrative.) There is no doubt that Duvernois felt the force of his narrative acutely, and might have written a very different story had he approached it in a more distant manner, in the vein of his cheerful comedies. It is a text that has more studied introspection in it than keen observation, and as such, is very much in the minority of the author's works. It is a story that probably makes its strongest appeal to people of much the same age as its author (60) and protagonist (56-59)—for the record, its translator was 61 when the work was done—but it can be appreciated well enough by anyone who has that milestone yet to reach, as well as those who have left it behind. It is, at any rate, a novel well worth reading, for its nutritional value as food for thought as well as its piquancy as a confection.

The edition I used for translation was the London Library's copy of the original edition, published by Bernard Grasset in 1936.

Brian Stableford

I.

Nothing, I should say straight away, predisposed me to be the hero of the adventure that you are about to read, and which is the most prodigious that any man has ever experienced.

I was born in Paris, in the heart of the Marais, on February 7, 1876. My name is Maxime-Félix Porte-reau—Maxime, thanks to my uncle and godfather, a wild boar they were trying to tame by endowing him with a godson; Félix, by virtue of a superstition of my parents who intended that I should be happy.

And I was happy, in fact, in the melancholy sense attributed by humans to the word. I was taking account of that one more time, on that afternoon in May 1832 which settled the direction of my destiny. I was alone in my study, where I did very little work but where tasted the most delicate joys: reading fine books, meditations populated with charming memories, perfumed visits…

A ray of sunlight had just replaced my friend Georgette. She had gone, and I was not at all grieved by it. When I was young and inexperienced, I would have tried to cage that pretty bird out of pride, but I was now at an age at which one doubts one's seductive abilities and at which one is, as charitable ladies put it, grateful for the slightest offering.

I do not believe that Georgette is interested, in the base sense of the term. No more do I believe that she is disinterested. She blushed with a great deal of grace when I slipped banknotes into her purse, but she left all the same, closing her full purse securely for fear of thieves. She would be incapable of giving herself for money, but she would also be incapable of giving herself to a pauper. The poor live in a world that she does not understand, and which frightens her. Her universe is restricted to certain elegant quarters, outside of which everything seems to be stench and darkness. She has the independence of ancient slaves, freed by a stroke of destiny, for whom remaining free constitutes the most cherished sensuality.

Married twice, she escaped once via widowhood and the second time by divorce, and has been, in consequence, the victim of three or four jealous lovers. I brought her indulgence, generosity, 30 years more than she had, and an unalterable politeness. Expelled from society by a scandal—her husband had pursued her with revolver shots—men treated her with a sort of excessive familiarity that humiliated her. The news-item had been circulated, and the ugliest and most timorous had not hesitated to make their cynical offers. She attracted me, with her fallen angel face, her limpid eyes ready for tears, her palely smiling mouth and her puerile hands, whose slight in-curved fingernails revealed a certain understanding of business...

I no longer feared that kind of enemy. I adopted her. Brunette, Georgette would not have pursued her career fruitfully; she chanced to be blonde, and lamented the fact. She would always find a refuge among mature gentlemen rendered paternal by fatigue.

She had arrived at my house in her car, so small that she jokingly called it "my scooter." There was scarcely room in it for her and a slender companion, but she had installed an enormous metal box containing rows of bottles of salts, perfumes, sweets, handbooks and two or three boring books whose pages were largely uncut.

Georgette lives in one of those livid streets in the vicinity of the Champs-Élysées, on the ground floor: a dwelling that would be ideal for a money-lender of it were not decorated with white and pink silks, illuminated by crystal and bathed in sweet odors. I had only gone into it two or three times, in passing. It is more convenient for me to see her in my own home. She knows the times when she is sure to find me there. Her arrival is almost always a pleasant surprise. I carefully incubate the vague desires that remain to me, which a regular cohabitation would quickly stifle. Georgette brings me a reflection of lost springtimes that I wasted. Her conversation amuses me, because it is out of the ordinary. When my mistress is not talking to me about her body, the choice foodstuffs she eats, the specialists who massage, polish and dress her, she embarks upon a terrified "It seems that they are in a dangerous state of mind in Germany?" or "it seems that business is not going well at present?" Her anguish appeals for optimistic responses that I hasten to lavish upon her. Certainly, she detests the poor, but I suspect her, by way of maintaining her euphoria and in the guise of an unimportant escapade, of maintaining a discreet liaison with a very young man, claimed during the weeks by his studies or employment in a department store, whom she must seek out on Saturday afternoons—her Sunday leisure-time being, she assures me too frequently, reserved for her family.

So, Georgette had arrived at 2 p.m., with the kind of assurance that hides an anxiety: "Is this the last time? Perhaps, in future, your faithful manservant Anselme will send me away, on the pretext that his master is ill or traveling?" She also fears an anonymous letter, an investigation: "I have learned something that has caused me pain…" I do not calm her immediately…one amuses oneself as one can. Ceremoniously, I kiss a hand that attempts to quiver at the contact of my lips; I offer an armchair, a fruit-juice; I address Georgette formally, and when I divine that her anxiety is at its height, I reassure her with a kiss, to which she responds with a passion derived from deliverance.

In fact, does she not give me all the love of which she is capable? I have seen her desperate, one day when our meeting unfolded entirely within my study. While chatting, I had let the moment pass when the dialogue between host and visitor expires, giving way to a silence that finds its denouement in more intimate surroundings. She would be equally furious if our conversations did not have a preliminary phase in my study. In fine weather, I break the ritual with a stroll in the country. My beautiful mistress leaves her scooter at my door. We install ourselves in my own car, driven by my chauffeur, Peutier, an honorable family man who hides beneath the most respectable exterior the disgust that my excesses inspire in him. Peutier keeps my testament in mind. He sometimes takes me to see his children, frightful gnomes who gaze at me like heirs. He fears that Georgette will collect my last sigh and important trinkets. He oscillates between hatred and a secret desire for association with the favorite.

Georgette has gone. I had lazily proposed an intimate dinner. She had declined my invitation. Had we not said all that we could say to one another and proved everything that we could prove to one another?

"The restaurant isn't good for my stomach," she sighed.

Thus, sparing my vanity, she takes to her own account everything that she secretly puts down to mine: if she finds me in a bad mood, she declares that she is ill, etc.

Having refused my offer, she buckled her belt, which bears her initials in large letters: G. G., Georgette Guillard. "Unless it would bore you to eat alone…?" she insinuated.

I made an evasive gesture, and she continued: "It's funny that you have no friends…" For she would not have refused the offer of a meal in the company of a dozen guests—male ones—in a brightly-lit place where she would have been enthroned in the place of honor, in front of a surfeit of pink carnations.

"Why don't you have any friends? I'm saying it for your benefit—you're amply sufficient for me, but you're so clever, such a good talker. It still astonishes me that you don't have at least one close friend…"

"I've had them. I could show you a drawer full of their photographs. Each one represents a treason or an unconfessed rancor that suddenly burst forth. As I detest hatred, I've renounced friendship. What I have left is love…"

She was ready, her hat on her head; she judged it appropriate to sit down again and murmured: "Love…oh yes…you're polite, treasure!"

I had retained from the time when I was sincere the duty of never separating from my mistress without putting, by means of affectionate and grateful words, a balm on the wound that physical love inflicts on a woman—even an unpolished and seemingly insensitive one. I therefore explained to Georgette all the delights, the most precise and the most ethereal, that I owed to her, and I detailed her charms, from the gilded ends of her hairs to the red tips of her slender fingernails. Such a speech moves her more reliably than music, however divine. Never speaking about oneself is clever, but is not speaking at length about one's partner, wisely, the best strategy?

"My darling!" Georgette exclaimed. "I'll dine with you!"

As I had no desire to do that, I mounted an assault of delicacy. To separate was, I affirmed, a refinement. To remain on a regret…not to drink her joy to the dregs…to think about one another…

In brief, I guided her amorously to the door. Still moved by my hymn to her beauty, she consented to disappear, to efface herself like a vision, with poetry and rapidity. Thus, thanks to protocol, we never went as far as familiarity, the mother of disputes.

"*Au revoir*, my only one!"

"*Au revoir*, my one and only!"

"Soon, the greatest of all little ones!"

That merciful ray of sunlight replaces Georgette at the appointed moment. It is as blonde as she is, and like her, it makes my dust dance in its scintillation…

I say "*Bonjour!*" to the gentle ray of sunlight. My manservant, who has just come in, takes that *bonjour* for himself and replies: "*Bonjour*, Monsieur. Is Monsieur feeling well?"

"Yes, thank you."

Anselme has played the Figaro to the sprightly Almaviva that I once was. He serves as a nanny to the old child that I have remained. He is bringing me a restorative brew, half strong black coffee and half thick chocolate—a recipe that he must have taken from Casanova, for he reads him avidly. "Monsieur should drink it hot," he advises me. "It would revive a dead man…"

A dead man? I look at myself in a mirror. It is the moment when the eyes still shine and the complexion is freshest, when kisses have effaced the wrinkles slightly…the one, finally, in which sensuality has wrought its change. Not bad: a distinguished baldness, a sort of tranquil strength, replacing the finesse of yesteryear…

"Will Monsieur be dining here?"

"I don't know…"

I don't have an interesting book to savor. I have singular preferences: I adore those old books that appeared between 1815 and 1880, which describe in great detail the Parisian life of restaurants, little theaters and pleasure spots. Thus, I know the Bois du Palais-Royal, the restaurateur Chevet, the Rocher de Cancale and the Bal Mabille better than our fashionable cabarets and the most up-to-date dance-halls. La Belle Limonadière, la Reine Pomaré, Rigolboche and Mogador have few secrets from me, and I know hidden corners—the Rue Saint-Roch, the Rue Saint-Honoré—where the dear past has not entirely finished dying…

But I had re-read that collection too many times, and knew it by heart.

Should I attend to my correspondence? I decided to leave it until tomorrow. My secretary, Mademoiselle Williamson, an old spinster who fished up her English name from God knows where, frees me from writing replies to borrowers, tax returns and so on…

Nevertheless, I picked up a letter to which I had not, since waking up, attached any importance. It was from one of my protégés, whom I had placed with my stockbroker, asking me to recommend him to a merchant of photographic apparatus: "I know that I will earn less, but I shall recover a fraternal friend, alongside whom I worked for more than ten years. I find myself so alone since his departure that I have no more enthusiasm for the work. I hope that your generosity will understand. I will give full and entire satisfaction to my new employer, as I have given full and entire satisfaction to the former..."

Georgette's words—"It's funny that you have no friends"—came back to me. The letter from this Montaigne of accountancy, explaining his affection for the La Boétie of photographic apparatus, enlightened me. Caught by the false semblances of facile *amour*, I had disdained amity. I almost missed my former relationships with comrades at college and in the regiment. No family, no friends. And when Georgette eventually disappears: solitude. I have been so persistent in refusing the invitations that the most tenacious have grown weary. "Portereau? He lives with a little woman and never leaves her side." I have been struck off all the aristocratic repertoires, and all the bourgeois memoirs. Besides, the society of men of my own age bores me; they have a mania for showing off their physical defects, exchanging medical prescriptions, pouring out vain recriminations or resigned laments. Younger ones only take any interest in me to ask for my assistance. Have I done enough for them? I wonder...

Yes, interesting myself in the young, following them, helping them...I shall find a means of sending this Orestes, mourning his Pylades, to the merchant of photographic apparatus.

And Anselme appears, with a finger to his lips and a tray in his hand, bearing a card and a letter. "I said, at hazard, that Monsieur was not seeing anyone."

I found myself in that state of mind in which one welcomes any diversion at all. The letter was from a former minister, my fellow on the board of a mining company, whose genuine talent as a caricaturist I had admired more than once when he reproduced, in the course of deadly meetings, the fallen faces of our colleagues. He recommended to me, with the warmest banality, the bearer of the missive, Monsieur Lucien Varvouste, a young man with a great future.

"Show him in."

"Monsieur won't reproach me?"

"No, no—show him in."

And Lucien Varvouste appeared. At his first words, which were mumbled to boot, I recognized this interlocutor dispatched by chance as a timid person. Now, I detest artful individuals, so I liked this Varvouste from the outset.

"Sit down, Monsieur."

"I wouldn't want to abuse…"

"Yes, yes—sit down…"

"I only require a minute…"

"Take your time. A cigarette?"

"No thank you, Monsieur."

"You don't smoke?"

"Not usually, Monsieur…"

Finally, he took one, in order not to seem rude. As he was trembling slightly, he did not succeed in uniting his cigarette with the flame, but he declared himself satisfied—"I'm lit"—and contented himself with chewing his cigarette, which he crumpled into a ball and threw underneath my desk when he thought that he was unobserved.

I deduced that he had torn himself away from his work and decided on this step in response to tender exhortations, and that his habitual negligence had been rectified by a woman's care. He was wearing a suit of a vulgar but proper cut. The poorly-effaced creases around the knot of his cravat, remade several time over, denoted patient labor. His black shoes, coarsely shaped, were polished dazzlingly. Anselme had not succeeded in dis-embarrassing him of a badly-folded umbrella, nor a hat of the shaggy variety, nor a portfolio in simulated morocco, dented at the corners. Tall in stature, but round-shouldered, he seemed to be about 30 years of age. His face interested me by virtue of its expressive ugliness. The same hands that had polished the shoes and retied the knot in the cravat ten times over had contrived a parting in thick red hair of the most commonplace sort, of which nothing remained but a few vestiges—but his eyes blazed behind his spectacles.

"I'll keep my gloves in," the stranger said, apologetically. "My fingers are so disfigured! To earn a living, I work as the second foreman in a garage. I have a wife, Monsieur, and two daughters, the elder six years old, the younger three. My wife is very considerate. I'm well aware that I am not providing her with the existence to which she has a right…but we're patient…"

"You're young."

"Yes, Monsieur, we're young, and we don't complain…"

He seemed suddenly to become aware of the abyss that separated these words from the real objective of his visit, and he experienced the terror of naïve lovers when they judge that the moment has come to risk a bold caress.

"I'm beginning to think," he stammered, "that I should not have come…I don't know where to begin…I think it might be better if I left. I might, for example, send you a detailed report…that's right, Monsieur, a report…When I say detailed…I am, all the same, the custodian of a secret…"

"I won't ask you to reveal your secret…"

"I'm quite ready to give it to you…but a paper that one entrusts to the mail…!"

"At least tell me what it's about."

"The gentleman who has been kind enough to recommend me to you thinks that I am in search of an active partner for some invention or other, like an improved shock-absorber or everlasting headlights…but it's something else entirely. Permit me to introduce myself. I'm originally from Châlons-sur-Saône. I've made rather extensive studies, especially in chemistry, physics and mechanics. My father and mother were both schoolteachers. That tells you what a struggle…! Ten years ago, I was forced to earn my living, with useless diplomas in my pocket. Mechanics attracted me. I'm not one of those people who thinks we're being destroyed by machinery, but I agree that we don't know how to make use of it.

"I found a place as a workman in a garage at Belleville, and I made the acquaintance of the person who became my wife. She worked in a small lingerie shop opposite the garage. We met in a café where she taught me which nutriments serve the body best, as they say. We were very serious. It seems that the young people of olden days were cheerful, but we've been forced to clench our fists. It's not that we scorn pleasure, but that we know nothing about it, not having the means…

"My employers considered me a bookish type, and no more, and advised me to follow a clerical career with a small pension at the end. To my parents, used to predicting the future of pupils, I had scarcely reaped the reward of my examinations. They came to Paris once. They saw me covered in grease, with oily hands, and they fled in alarm. My wife was the first to discern in me something other than a well-meaning imbecile. Perhaps I really am nothing but an imbecile—but one who has had an idea…just one, Monsieur! Except that, as soon as it surged forth, it took entire possession of me. I'm an imbecile who has had an idea, therefore, and will follow it through to the end…I shall never have another; this one is sufficient…"

His chest swelled and he tried to catch his breath, as if his own glory were choking him. At that moment, he seemed handsome: grotesque and handsome. Already, he was continuing: "It might be that I'm mistaken. My invention is on paper. The definitive realization will be very onerous. But there is an intermediate phase: a trial, for which I need 20,000 francs and three months of tranquility. I've come to you without any great hope, Monsieur. I'm asking you to throw 20,000 francs into an experiment that has eight chances in ten of failing—but I swear to you that the two remaining chances are worth the trouble…"

He murmured the rest fervently: "To go from one point to another with the speed of light…Difficult? Impossible? But little inventions, Monsieur, like wireless telegraphy, for example, or even the cinema, appeared chimerical at first…"

He stopped, afraid of having said too much. He mopped his brow and, as he had taken off his spectacles, I was struck by the brightness of his eyes, to which he was trying to return a smile, but which were still burning with the evocation of his discovery.

"Hold on, Monsieur," I said, taking pity. "Have some of this: coffee and chocolate mixed. Please…"

I was thinking: *He's probably a madman, but perhaps he's also a genius. His idea might, perhaps end up as an electric train set for children under 13, but a singer starting out wants to be Virgil, and a good officer dreams of being Bonaparte. If he's not merely deluded, or indecisive, this boy is a force—a modest force, a force of our era—but a force nevertheless.*

"Would you care to come to my place on Sunday, at 2 p.m.?" he murmured. "It's a long way away, in a wretched neighborhood, but I'd be able to explain to you, show you my plans…"

I agreed to the meeting.

"If you haven't arrived by 3 p.m.," Varvouste concluded, "I'll understand. Oh, Monsieur, I'll understand, and I won't hold it against you. I thank you, in any case, for your welcome. You're the first person I've approached. I didn't dare. It's my wife who pushed me… She'll be happy when I go back and tell her what's happened, even if we don't reach a successful conclusion…"

"Rely on me—2 p.m. on Sunday."

He thanked me again and went out, mumbling, bowing, bumping into corers, carrying his false morocco portfolio, his badly-rolled umbrella…and a marvelous hope.

II.

On Sundays, I give my servants the day off. Does Georgette dedicate the day to her family? I had never tried to resolve that enigma. When I was young, I had the mania of believing that I was adored; now that I was mature, I no longer believe that I'm loved. Perhaps I'm still mistaken...

My mistress ought to be in some suburban villa, visiting a father and a mother to whom she brings the kind of cake fashionable among little folk, a bouquet of flowers and some shag tobacco for a pipe. As for Peutier the chauffeur, he is loading himself into a taxi with his obese wife and hideous children, and giving technical advice to his colleague. Professional prejudice!

For myself, if time permits, I go on foot to a restaurant near the Madeleine, where I find a few bachelors of my generation. They eat there, each at his little table, between newspapers that give them news of a universe in which they no longer participate and plates full of food that they eye suspiciously. The most valiant among them go to a theater afterwards, to pass severe judgment on contemporary literature and its interpretation. They have retained a species of gaiety, proof of their unconsciousness. Some, whom I know, wish me a small conspiratorial *bonjour*. We do not amalgamate. Those who still drink a small glass of Armagnac after their dessert gaze ironically at the gastralgics devoted to tea. The alcoholics think: *They're done for all the same!* The tea drinkers think: *At the rate he's going, that idiot hasn't got much time left!* And they all feel a sense of superiority.

The idea of seeing them again discouraged me. I went past the restaurant without stopping, to the great surprise of the porter preparing to roll out the barrel, and I took to the great boulevards—or, rather, what remains of the great boulevards. The weather was very pleasant—the kind that Providence reserves for the Sunday leisure of Parisians. I arrived without fatigue in the Place de la République.

It was 1:30 p.m. I decided to grab a hasty meal in a restaurant near the garage whose address Lucien Varvouste had given me. I chose a deserted little brasserie. The only waiter took his time getting to me, as if he wanted to advise me to take my custom elsewhere, but the pace was clean. I spotted a table in a sort of bow-window that isolated me from the big room, and through which I could contemplate the bustle of the street.

I had scarcely finished the *hors-d'oeuvres* when I was surprised to see Georgette come in, so far from our distinguished quarters—a Georgette disguised, one might have said, as a little seamstress, rejuvenated, as rosy as spring, and accompanied, of course, by a charming young man.

In the rage that gripped me, I recognized the jealousy of old. After an exercise of will-power, I soon felt nothing but pity. Georgette had no suspicion that the patient edifice of so many months had crumbled! The couple went straight to a habitual corner, which I could observe without being seen. She huddled up to the young man amiably and guided him in the consultation of the menu. Doubtless she was choosing the cheapest dishes. When he tried to put his arm around her she gave him a mischievous slap on the wrist and returned to the examination of the menu. I was tempted to call the waiter and say: "Tell that lady and gentleman not to worry, because the old man will pay…" Facile! Too easy!

I hastened to eat my cutlet, with no appetite. I paid the bill. Then, as I had noticed a door let into the bow-window, I had the unused door opened, and escaped, only having awakened the curiosity of the cashier and the waiter.

A third sensation: exile! Certainly, the scene that had just been offered to me told me nothing that I had not anticipated, but the truth provokes unexpected reactions. Mine was this: *What am I doing in all this? What am I doing in life? I distribute, according to the whims of my egotism, the money of which I am the custodian. I am the treasurer of my fantasies. I walk around like those strangers who fall into the joyful animation of a city in which they feel themselves to be intruders…*

Exile.

Varvouste, dressed in his new suit with his hair laboriously vaselined, was waiting for me in front of his garage. A man was washing a car, of the sort that one sees abandoned in scrap-yards.

"In this good weather," Varvouste said to me, "cars of every possible sort are out and about."

He took me through a yard in which there was a shed flanked by three little rooms. The first served as a dining-room and bedroom. "Unfortunately, it's a little damp." He called out: "Celia!"

Madame Varvouste appeared, her hat on her head, pushing two kids in front of her, whom she was instructing to be polite to the gentleman, and who tried to smile at me. She seemed to me to be prey to the anxiety of spouses who believe their husbands to be victims of obsession. Beneath her amiability I discerned a vague reproach—something akin to: "You're not going to encourage him!"—and also the dread of seeing me disperse the accumulated phantasms with a brutal refusal.

"You'll find fresh cider on the sideboard, and grenadine syrup, if Monsieur doesn't like cider. I'm taking the children to the Buttes-Chaumont. We won't be back before 6 p.m…"

"All right, all right!" Varvouste muttered, impatiently.

I kissed the children on their cheeks. I shook the feverish hand of the poor woman, whose prettiness had faded. Already, Varvouste was bringing out plans, notebooks covered in writing and figures.

"This," he announced, "is what will turn the human world upside-down…"

III.

Varvouste has solved the problem of inter-atomic energy. It is as simple as that! That is to say that he has taken to its extreme limit the attempts at liberation sketched out by radium—and thanks to his discovery, an interplanetary voyage will become possible. In three years one could reach, in the direction of the nearest star to Earth, Proxima Centauri, a planet to which Varvouste has given the name of his wife, Celia. The first attempt might perhaps be made with a reduced apparatus—a sort of rocket—which would be followed by a large shell containing everything that a human being would need to live inside it for months...

It's imbecilic.

At 6 p.m., worn-out with fatigue, and prey to a violent headache, I declared; "You have the elements of a curious book...a popular romance...You ought to begin with a book."

Madame Varvouste came back in at this point. She murmured: "I've given him that advice so often..."

"Not you, Celia," the unfortunate begged. "Come on, not you! I don't do literature, but science, and the most practical..."

"I'll willingly put 20,000 francs at your disposal," I proposed, "since that sum will suffice for a trial."

"And if the trial succeeds," Madame Varvouste whimpered, "he'll want to go...he'll go through with this madness, you see!"

I repeat that I had a very bad headache. I pronounced the following words, which slipped out and which, by virtue of a bizarre duplication, I heard with admiring astonishment as if they came from someone else: "Don't worry. I'll be the one to go. I've got nothing to lose. Not only do I promise, I make it the express condition of my partnership. A little voyage to…to…"

"Proxima Centauri," Varvouste supplied.

"…wouldn't displease me. You can guarantee my return?"

"If you reach Proxima Centauri, you'll be attracted by the planet Celia, and I'll come to look for you if you can't get back by yourself. It would only take me six months to construct a new apparatus, if you leave me the material possibility of doing so."

I raised another objection. "Your discovery must have other consequences than such a long journey. Couldn't we envisage some immediate applications?"

"No. Later, no doubt. Today, my work can only be fully applied by moving outside our atmosphere and bathing in radiation that is only found in unexplored regions. Besides, my invention will only bring about a trivial progress in aviation. To test a submarine it's necessary to descend…"

"Here, it's necessary to rise…"

"It is indeed."

After that we talked about the different and wretched problems that afflict our poor Earth, and I went out uttering the relieved "oof!" of a reasonable man who has spent his afternoon listening to a feverish one—but I had almost forgotten Georgette and my rival.

That was well worth 20,000 francs.

Strangely enough, nothing interests me anymore but this. Varvouste has drawn me in his wake, up into the clouds. I've seen Georgette again. I received her in my study. I had 300,000 francs in banknotes in front of me.

"Are you doing your accounts?" she asked me, in a slightly faltering voice

"Yours."

"Mine? I don't understand."

"Take it…"

"I'm to take it?"

"Yes. Take it away. Make a parcel. Hold on— here's paper and string…"

"A gift?"

"I'm going away."

"I don't want it, then…"

"I'm going away, Georgette."

"Where are you going?"

"Far away."

"And you're leaving me?"

"Invest this money in an annuity."

"I refuse your money."

"Thank you."

"Another woman, presumably?"

"Georgette, we've never discussed…"

"What do you mean by *discussed*?"

Do you want this liaison, charming in so many ways, to end in shouting, lying and tears?"

"I want to know…"

"Knowing is so painful, alas! I assure you—I'm speaking from experience. My darling, let's not spell anything out. Let's leave things imprecise. What does it all matter, from the viewpoint of Proxima Centauri?"

"Translate, I beg you."

"There, the parcel is made up. Go, and don't come back."

"You haven't even kissed me."

"I prefer to retain the memory of our last kiss."

Her face is genuinely distressed, but the hands with the incurved fingernails are ready to take the parcel all the same, and hold on tight. "In sum, you're leaving me?"

"In sum, we're separating."

"There are things you ought to know…"

"Shh!"

"It's not true…" And, on the threshold, this candid admission: "In any case, no woman—you hear, not one—will ever love you more than I do…"

"I'm convinced of it—and that's what breaks my heart."

She searches for a riposte, finds none, and leaves. Varvouste's first success: the liberation of atoms… The trial rocket will not depart any more rapidly than Georgette has just departed, with her 300,000 francs, sprinkled with tears, perhaps not all of which are tears of happiness…

The rocket is ready. It looks like an ostrich egg equipped with minuscule winglets. Inside, there's a message from an inhabitant of the Earth. One turn of the key of a mechanical toy, and the egg will fly away…or ought to fly away. We shall see…

June 2, midnight. Varvouste and I have come to the Bois de Boulogne. We have arrived in the vicinity of the Bagatelle. We had to wait; amorous couples disturbed us. Finally, the moment has come. A throbbing roar. The rocket scintillates joyfully, as if it were freed from all known attachments. It's out of sight already.

"It'll get there, I'm sure of it!" murmurs Varvouste. And he throws himself into my arms, weeping…

"An accident?" asks a passer-by, full of solicitude.

"No, no," I say. "Monsieur is emotional."

"I understand!"

The sky is now overcast. It is starting to rain. I bring back a delirious Varvouste, convinced that he has just communicated with the Unknown...

So far as the world is concerned, we have constructed an aircraft, the technicians of which think it nothing extraordinary. We have resolved to keep the whole thing secret. In case of failure, we'll begin again. If we succeed, we have to surprise the world. I'm convinced. It's a case of *folie à deux*.

Madame Varvouste only sees one thing: I'm leaving without her husband. She will keep him by her side, with his children. For me, is it a suicide? Yes and no. I've spent long nights contemplating the stars. Little by little, my personality has become detached. A prodigy has been realized: I'm no longer thinking about myself. I knew similar intervals during the war. I just thought: *All this is absurd. It's abject horror, and I don't want to save my skin.* And shortly afterwards, because a breath of wind had passed by, a perfume of France enveloped in music, I no longer thought that skin so precious. A sort of inspiration lifted me up; the coward mutated into a hero...

What excites me most is that I shall be alone. A few kilometers from this globe, doubtless imperfect, but comfortable in the meantime, I shall very probably die of asphyxia in my prison. I have every chance dying, and dying obscurely. Varvouste affirms that he has thought of everything: a reservoir of water that will be renewed automatically thanks to a procedure known to him alone—so much for thirst; for hunger, I'm taking enough concentrated nutriments to sustain me for several years, provided that I don't get greedy. I have the necessary provisions of breathable air and enough space, cleverly organized, to permit me to exercise my muscles. I'm running no risk of starvation, thirst or paralysis. Besides, my health is excellent and the doctors to whom I have declared that I'm going to take a long trip in an aircraft have not raised any opposition. I enjoy, it appears, a magnificent heart, magnificent blood-pressure, a magnificent stomach…

Am I afraid?

The time of reckoning is approaching. Still the sentiment experienced during attacks: *It's insane, but I'm sure I'll get out of it.* I merely observe a singular dryness of the mouth. My tongue sticks to my palate. I need to drink incessantly or suck pastilles. No shadow of hesitation. What is certain is that a vaudevillesque incident— the treason of a woman that I didn't even love—has cut the last tie. If I recoil at the last moment, if I refuse to let myself be dispatched like a parcel in the problematic direction of Proxima Centauri, I'm capable, out of weariness and self-disgust of ending it all by a shop-girl's suicide.

In our epoch, going to China would be like a trip to the suburbs. I've acquired a taste for adventure. Either I shall leave a name immortal in human memory, or I'll be volatilized. It might also be that I shall arrive in a marvelous country and will disdain to give my news to the unfortunates who continue to crawl on the surface of our globe, or that I'll come back, having not left the apparatus, bringing back observations, photographs and the key to the great mystery, having learned to live there as a bird lives with its wings, eventually to share with Varvouste an unprecedented glory.

No, it really is a matter of suicide. The Georgette incident, insignificant in itself, has opened my eyes. I'm one of those people who don't know how to grow old, or, if you prefer, I'm one of those people who can only live their youth. All the rest has been nothing but a succession of failures. I pass judgment very lucidly on what I have been, as if it were someone else. I make allowances for parental exaggeration, but it was the rule, around me, to credit me with genius. Genius, no—without doubt—but sufficiently bright talents and a sensibility that was bound to fade away rapidly, before the age of 25.

Before certain events that made our fortune, my family was poor. In our little house in the Rue des Archives, there was no piano. A relative, having bought a "baby grand," gave us his upright piano. I was six years old at the time. The arrival of that luxurious and sonorous item of furniture dazzled me. Six months later, vaguely instructed by a professor at a discount, I was tapping out little symphonies of my own invention. A composer cried prodigy and, taking me in his arms, cried: "I'm hugging Mozart!" I made progress, but three years later, on the pretext that his daughter needed an instrument, the relative took the piano back. I shed tears when men as lugubrious as undertakers carried off my vocation. And later, when my father was able to buy a baby grand, the action of an old egotist had killed my inspiration. I wrote verses then, which I tore up afterwards, which were doubtless imperfect but which marked the birth of a poet. I modeled fine statuettes in wax. One of my dullard friends drew targets on the paper in my bedroom, made bullets of my wax and used them as projectiles. I possessed oratorical gifts; I could convince people. A prolix intelligence, I admit, but prodigious gifts. I deposited them at the feet of silly girls. In youth, I betrayed my marvelous childhood. Later, I betrayed my youth. I retain a remorse that still stabs at me…everything that I might have been starved in satiation!

In reality, I have been dead for 30 years. I cherish the child, the adolescent and the young man that I was and whom no one understood. The rest is not even worth a regret. At any rate, to rehabilitate my dismal old age I shall have an exploit: a crazy exploit, but an exploit!

I have renounced the contemplation of the sky. Proxima Centauri no longer interests me. It is, it seems, my fatherland that I'm going to rejoin. I'm attached to the pettiest aspects of the Earth in general, and Paris in particular. They seem touching…

My affairs are in order. I've left a large sealed envelope to be opened after three years absence—the legal interval. Varvouste, his wife and children will be protected. I've let my domestics go, telling them that I'm going abroad, but that I might possibly return. I've studied the apparatus that will carry me away until I'm sick of it. I still have a week to kill…seven centuries, seven hours…

A beautiful night. The stars are fraternal…their palpitation seems to be calling me. Madame Varvouste is here. She dreads that her husband might decide at the last minute to accompany me. He is unhappy: "You're playing the better part," he assures me. She thinks she'll get him back once I'm gone. It is midsummer, but I'm very cold. I speak calmly, even good-humoredly, but in a jerky fashion. And still that unbearable dryness in my mouth…

I've had a copious meal—my last on Earth. I've drunk two bottles of champagne and one of old brandy, without getting drunk.

There's no one on the airfield.

I'm installed; the door closes…

A dull explosion…

Gone!

IV.

My scientific observations can be found in the accompanying notebook. Here, I'm only recording my impressions. The apparatus is not under my control. It's
obeying the force that launched it. I'm prey to an ardent
curiosity. I've already passed the limit assigned to ex-
plorers of the stratosphere. I'm traveling through a new
radiance, phases of incandescent pink and molten silver.
Thought is no longer as rapid. I'm ceasing to think. I
change the day on my calendar. I exercise my muscles. I
consult the reservoir of water, which is indeed refilling
automatically. I swallow alimentary tablets. And I go to
sleep. I only dread one thing: suddenly being gripped by
terror.

I didn't anticipate the impatience. After two
months, it has taken hold of me. I surprise myself by
murmuring: "Enough! I'm going back." It's like that old
lady tapping with her umbrella on the back of her
coachman, who is trying in vain to hold back two stam-
peding horses, shouting: "Slow down, Auguste, or I'll
fire you!" Varvouste warned me that he couldn't guarantee the return maneuver. I suspect him of having rigged
the apparatus, to forestall any cowardice on my part. Re-
leasing the switch didn't alter my course by a centimeter.
I'm still rising. There's nothing to do but resign myself
to it.

A week of inertia, of prostration…

I hate Varvouste. He just had to fall into my life! As
for me, I never showed enough gratitude with regard to
that peaceful, protected life in which the whole world
worked for me, where I was never projected into space

like an insect in a seashell…breakfast brought by the faithful Anselme…a leisurely morning among the books and the newspapers…and Georgette, decorated and perfumed, Georgette, who brought me, after all, the illusion of love…and the streets…and the shops…

This blind projection into darkness! The instrument that's carrying me, it's just the same as staying on Earth, on the divine Earth for which I was made, and snuggling up there in a soft nest. Why has destiny chosen me, the most placid and skeptical of men? I'm no longer moving. My beard has grown. The last of my hair is coming away in handfuls. My mirror sends back the haggard image of a terrified old man, and I'm falling into a bottomless sleep.

I wake up cured. I've opened a porthole. I breathe in a sort of delight—the lightness and *joie de vivre* that one finds on the highest mountains. I have light at my disposal. I take advantage of it to shave. I recover a plausible, familiar face. I'm no longer traveling with that terror-stricken stranger. I make my joints click. Intact. I have two balls to send out. I'll send one of them with my first observations, a note addressed to Varvouste. On the first railway journey, the travelers were obliged to pass through these alternations. The journey from Paris to Proxima Centauri will soon be familiar. Let us put on a brave face for posterity…

Anyway, Maxime-Félix Portereau, what would you have done with your old carcass? You would have continued to care for it by delivering it to the undertakers. The fate that is reserved for you is far more enviable?

Varvouste was right to prevent me from turning back. It seems that I'm on a stable plane. The anticipations of science are doubtless mistaken. There was mention of three light-years, but I'm borne by favorable waves, as if attracted by a magnet. Perhaps I'll gain time. I shall arrive. Where? I have no idea, but I shall arrive.

What does it matter anyway? I'm no longer the representative of Earth. I belong to this intoxicating atmosphere, this enchanted night, brighter than day.

And the Sun is no longer anything but a large star...

I've been ill—very ill. Drink, swallow five or six pills, consult my dials, strike off the days on the calendar...I was incapable of anything else.

In spite of everything, one thing is sure: the certainty of seeing something that no one has seen before. To glimpse it and disappear, carrying away the secret for which I won't have paid dear...

Months added to months. I've never felt better. My illness was caused by an abscess in my leg. I've lanced the abscess, and taken care of myself. When I can, I do my Swedish gymnastics. I wash myself carefully. I don't know where my cadaver will come to rest, but I want that cadaver to do me honor.

I've brought books. I've tried to read—in vain. I no longer understand the sentences that once enchanted me. I sense therein all the weakness of human thought. I'm in a region where the writing no longer corresponds to anything.

And after the fiery night, something that resembles an aurora. A troubled rosiness, a naïve rose after those roses of flame, a rose that I know...the light at the end of the tunnel? An illusion...a mirage...? Perhaps I'm senile...

Indeed…the night returns, but heavy… I've been in flight for two years and 11 months, and for the first time, the apparatus hesitates. The rebel handle obeys me…

Descent…

I was in a cloudy night…

O marvel, here comes the day!

I can see trees…

The planet Celia has trees, life…it's populated… Mountains, minuscule houses…

The apparatus is hovering…

Stupidly, I shout: "Come and find me! Hello! I'm a man" Here's a man! A man from Earth!"

A shock…flames. The apparatus touches down on the planet. Celia is volatilized. I've arrived—but my clothes are on fire. I tear them off. I'm naked, but for a leather belt, having nothing but that belt and a winged ball that I was able to save.

May 2, 1935, 6 a.m…

Where am I?

With burns on my face, my hands, my breast and my feet, I'm in atrocious agony. A forest…an inhabited forest, with a well-worn path. I breathe in a strong perfume of resinous trees, mingled with the odor of wood cooking-fires.

"Help!"

I'm thirsty. My tongue is stuck to my palate again. All curiosity has vanished. I want a drink, that's all.

A man…

A man reminiscent of our peasants. He's an old man with a white beard. He questions me, in a language I don't understand, a guttural, language similar to German. He shakes his head. He makes a sign bidding me to wait. And I faint…

I woke up in a sort of farmhouse. I was lying down. A doctor was examining me. He smiled at me. I smiled at him.

"French!" I said. "An inhabitant of Earth!"

He made a sign telling me that he understood, and another demanding a little patience. On his instructions, milk, vegetable soup and fresh water were brought. I had to sleep for twenty-four hours. After that, the bearded old man showed me a starched shirt and a black rustic Sunday suit, and indicated by gestures that I should get dressed.

A young woman with blonde plaits, more robust than pretty, but cheerful and attractive, served as my nurse. She passed her hand over my face to signify that she felt sorry for me, and showed me the fine clothes.

With my head swathed in cotton wool and my left leg bandaged, I put on the shirt with no cravat and the suit.

And the door opened…

I recognized as soon as he spoke that I was dealing with a civil servant. He was wearing a morning-coat and a bowler hat, equipped with a proud moustache, and was brandishing papers.

"Are you French, Monsieur?" he said to me.

"Yes, Monsieur."

"I too am French, an attaché at the consulate."

"Oh? There is a France, and consulates?"

"Yes, of course, Monsieur. Can you explain to me the sequence of events that led to your being found naked and badly burned in Kahlenberg Forest?"[1]

"I'm in Kahlenberg Forest?"

"Exactly."

"What country, exactly?"

"Austria-Hungary."

"Austria?"

"Hungary."

"Please excuse me, Monsieur, but I'm experiencing considerable confusion."

"I can see that; you're entirely excused."

"Might I be permitted to ask you a few questions, which will doubtless seem foolish to you?"

"Please do, Monsieur; I shall reply to you as obligingly as I shall expect you to do in a little while, when I interrogate you."

"We are, you tell me in Austria-Hungary?"

"Yes, still!"

"And under what regime does that country live?"

"Under the reign of His Majesty the Emperor Franz-Josef."

"What is the date?"

"May 2."

"In what year?"

"1896! You have, indeed, suffered a shock!"

"Monsieur, I have a revelation to make to you. I beg you to observe that I am not speaking under the influence of a fever. I will bring to what I am about to tell

---

[1] Kahlenberg is a mountain overlooking the city of Vienna; the forest on its slopes is more commonly known as the Wiener-wald.

you all desirable precision. In brief, here it is: my name is Maxime-Félix Portereau…"

"Are you related to the Adrien Portereau who painted rural scenes in the 1840s?"

"He was my grandfather."

"We are in familiar territory, then. In my parents' dining-room in Limoges there are some sheep signed by Adrien Portereau. A pretty painting, full of taste and sentiment…"

"I congratulate you, Monsieur. I see that you have not fallen into the snares of contemporary taste, such as cubism…"

"What?"

"Excuse me. You can't imagine, Monsieur, the magnitude of what I have to tell you. I'll do so very rapidly. Having subsidized one of our compatriots, named Varvouste, I took my place two and a half years ago in a machine of his invention, which travels through space at the speed of light…"

"I think that I had better let you rest for a while…"

"Oh, I understand your incredulity, Monsieur. For near three years I have been traveling in that shell. Having departed on July 3, 1932…"

"Ah!"

"Yes, Monsieur."

"And how have you survived during that time?"

"I shall explain. Besides, even though the apparatus caught fire, debris will doubtless be found that will inform scientists… Suddenly, I saw daylight, trees, and houses. I thought that I had been returned to Earth by some unknown miracle, for my control mechanisms had not ceased functioning. I was in reality, as I have the honor of informing you that you are, on the planet Celia, and that what you doubtless call the Sun…"

"Yes, that is the name that we give to that star…"

"…Is none other than the star Proxima Centauri."

"But we can easily see Proxima Centauri from here on clear nights—it's the closest star to us, as all the astronomers will tell you.[2] You'll understand, Monsieur, that your story leaves me slightly skeptical. So you left the Earth—your Earth—on July 3, 1932, and you arrive here on May 2, 1896. Strange!"

"Don't ask me to explain, Monsieur. Perhaps all inhabited planets reproduce one another exactly, with a time-lag of a few years one way or the other."

"Which means that there will, at this moment, be a young Portereau in Paris who is none other than yourself?"

"Myself at the age of 20, Monsieur—and I shall not see him without experiencing a poignant emotion."

"Which is understandable—but Monsieur, you spoke just now about proofs."

"I'll give you all you could desire. For instance, I can predict great events that will be realized in every detail. Extraordinary things have happened in the world. France has gone through a frightful war between 1914 and 1918. Germany and Austria-Hungary, defeated…"

"Later, Monsieur, if you please. I would prefer immediate proofs."

---

[2] This does not make sense, for if Celia were a planet of "our" Proxima Centauri, Earth's Sun, as seen from there, would be at a point in the firmament directly opposite the constellation Centaurus. The "mistake" may be deliberate, intended to line up with various subtler clues indication that this entire sequence is hallucinatory, the "starship" never having left the vicinity of Earth.

"My papers have been destroyed. Fortunately, I still have this belt, in which I have 10,000 francs in gold. You can look at the dates on the coins."

Hastily, I unfastened my belt. I opened the pocket and observed that the most recent of the coins bore the date 1892, the others bearing the effigy of Napoleon III.

"In any case," my interlocutor concluded, "what you have told me is so singular—let's not mince words, so extraordinary—that it surpasses my understanding and my authority. If you feel sufficiently well, I would like you to come with me to Vienna."

"Right away, of course!"

"I shall put you in touch with and attaché at the embassy who will take you to His Excellency the French Ambassador."

"And then to His Majesty?"

"Perhaps, Monsieur."

"I would be able to give him useful advice."

"I'm convinced of it. I'll ask these good people to lend you a cloak…"

We arrived, in mid-afternoon, in a beautiful park, on the far side of which I saw a house of rather rugged appearance, which astonished me in that charming and cheerful Vienna.

My companion showed me into a reception-room. "Wait here a moment," he said. "You'll be received by His Excellency's first and second secretaries." He shook my hand and went out.

As if they had been waiting for his signal, two men in smocks came in, threw themselves upon me, and led me away.

I was in a madhouse. While they put me under the shower, I thought that I deserved no better, and that if anyone had addressed a speech like mine to me, I would not have hesitated to put him in the hands of an alienist. I must say that, considering the state I was in, still suffering from burns and exhausted by privations, the shower nearly dispatched me to a better world—to the definitive planet that cannot reproduce any of the ridiculous existent planets.

From excitement, I passed to stupidity. I was left to rest.

The next day, the doctor in charge, followed by interns and representatives of the police, came to ask me through the medium of an interpreter whether I still believed that I had been sent from another planet to give certain warnings to the one on which I found myself.

I replied that I could not remember the more-or-less incoherent words that had escaped me during a violent confusion, that I felt better, but in such a state of weakness that my amnesia was complete. I could no longer remember my name or my nationality…

"Have me sent back to France," I said, "and I am sure that my memories will come back to me in abundance."

He nodded his head, in a sign of vague assent, and confided me to a male nurse, who plunged me back into my sheets and tucked me in with such brutality that I felt that I was in a straitjacket.

I have thought of a plausible story. I left Paris in a balloon whose tethering rope was worn and which broke—and, delivered to the whims of the wind, I landed in Kahlenberg. I tell the story to everyone. I have been taken out of my room and placed in a communal dormitory. I am able to exchange observations with a companion in misfortune, who thinks that he is an angel and hardly ever moves, in order to preserve his wings from any impure contact. I have one exceedingly cheerful neighbor who utters loud bursts of laughter, and a lugubrious one who raises his tearful eyes to Heaven incessantly, putting his hands together…

A month goes by. My burns heal. I put on weight.

One morning, the interpreter comes back. He checks my health. Then he informs me that, the administrative formalities having been completed, I will soon be sent back to my native land, with the hope that I will recover my memory there.

I shall see once again all the dear individuals that I believed lost forever. I shall find myself. I shall find the 20-year-old Maxime Portereau, my double, myself!

I burst into sobs.

"Some good advice," the interpreter whispers. "Don't weep too much. It seems that it's not a good sign, from the cerebral point of view. Hold yourself together, and least until you get home. As for the rest, imagine that you've had a nightmare…"

V.

Every man, whether he hardens himself or not, whether he tries to move forward or consumes himself in regrets, belongs to the epoch in which he was young. In the train that is taking me back to my 20th year, I gaze indifferently at the star that was my former sun. It seems to me that I am going home after a 40-year absence.

I left the asylum in the company of an individual who combined the functions of guard and nurse, who had been instructed to accompany me to the frontier. He was a fly in the ointment. I took ten fine *louis* from the 10,000 francs that constituted my entire fortune, which I offered to him on condition that he let me leave on my own. He would keep the price of his ticket as a bonus. He would only have to declare, subsequently, that he had taken me to the designated place and handed me over to the competent authorities. I tried to explain myself with the aid of a dictionary and by pantomime. He understood, and seemed quite delighted with the idea of a holiday. At the barber's shop where I had my hair trimmed, I provided him with a haircut and a perfumed lotion. Then I bought a traveling suit, a bowler hat and an ample overcoat; I bought a green felt hat for my companion and had the feeling that I was fulfilling his most secret desire.

On the platform at the railway station he asked for his fee, making signs to inform me that he would leave me to my own devices. I gave him the ten gold coins. He thanked me, clicked his heels, raised his new hat and concluded: "Gutby, M'sieu. Dake care!"

"Ja! Take care!" Then I stopped short. "Hey! I have no passport!"

"Nicht passport?"

It was true. I was having a certain difficulty in persuading myself that I was really living in 1896. In 1896, that formality seemed unnecessary. A fortunate epoch, when one lived the good life…although it is true that, for the people of the First Empire, the good life had expired under Louis XV…

My guard wanted to keep up appearances. He turned away to study a poster. I made myself scarce.

If I "took care," and abstained from any prediction of the future, if I did not take the risk of telling the story, no matter how reasonably, of my implausible adventure, I would become, little by little, the richest and most glorious man on the planet Celia…

And I would keep my secret from everyone—except, perhaps, Mama…

I had been thinking aloud. At the word "mama," pronounced with fervent tenderness by a grey-haired old man, a young woman looked at me in amazement, laughing. I adopted my most serious expression. I was not yet out of danger…

The train…how slow it is, for a man who had recently been traveling at 300,000 kilometers per second!

Fortunately, I am alone in a modest second-class compartment—but an intruder is coming in. Some Austro-Hungarian policeman who is going to take me back to a prison-asylum? No. He bows to me, deposits a suitcase in the luggage-rack, sits down, checks the time on his watch and say: "Nach Paris?"

"Yes, Monsieur," I reply. "I'm going to Paris."

He rubs his hands. "I'd have laid odds that you were French, in spite of the costume! You bought that suit and coat in Vienna, didn't you? I knew, that, being in the business myself, Auguste Estivoque, children's clothing, Rue d'Uzès."

I bow. Auguste Estivoque waits momentarily for me to inform him in my turn, but I remain silent. He does not persist. He wants to chat, though. He is a small man with a friendly face and a pot-belly.

"I adore journeys," he tells me. "I could avoid them, because I have very conscientious traveling salesmen, but it's stronger than I am—I have to check things out for myself. I take advantage of it to enrich my collection of photographs. Here, Monsieur, look at my most recent works. Here's a rather nice Prater, and a Schoenbrunn.[3] It's not as good as our Champs-Elysées. How long has it been since you left France?"

"Quite a long time…"

"You're probably disgusted, like me. At our age, one only asks for tranquility. A dream, alas! No one is sure of anything any longer…"

He chats about current affairs: the Arton scandal, the blackmail trial following the death of a young millionaire, and foreign affairs too: the Adua disaster; Monsieur Crispi's resignation. I feel that I'm in the process of riffling through the yellowing archives of a newspaper.[4]

---

[3] The Wiener Prater park and the Schoenbrunn Palace are still two of Vienna's leading tourist attractions—exactly the sort of thing of which a pioneer of that dubious art would be taking snapshots in 1896.

[4] Which is presumably what Duvernois did by way of research. Emile Arton was one of eight députés involved in a

"How will it all end?" my neighbor sighs

"Quite well!" And, returning to the prudence that must be my law, I add: "Probably...for I'm no seer..."

He too is optimistic. Thus, he has a blind confidence in Wilhelm II. "I know what I'm talking about. I sometimes went to Berlin at one time, and I was received there like a prince. Then again, I have a relative who is very well placed in the Ministry of Foreign Affairs. The Kaiser's only ambition is peace. I know that he celebrated the anniversary of 1870 with a great military fête—I call that throwing off ballast. It's necessary to satisfy the general staff, but that doesn't prevent him from acting gently. I can give you some inside information—you can take advantage of it, if you're interested in the Bourse, but keep it to yourself. There's no question of giving Wilhelm II the Légion d'Honneur, of course—no, the Légion d'Honneur would bring back bad memories, and that wouldn't be wise... Good! But he's just sent us a gift: a copy of a painting he's done himself: *The Struggle of Civilization against the Yellow Race*. He's interested in art, and he doesn't mind putting his hand to work. At the inauguration of the last Salon, you know, he was annoyed, very annoyed. He had a very high opinion of painting: he doesn't like the rules being broken. And do you know what the empress said? She said: 'These painters are crazy! They persist in not fol-

---

massive financial fraud in 1892 involving the funding of the Panama Canal; he skipped the country but was brought back in 1896 to face trial. The battle of Adua, Adwa, or Adowa, at which Ethiopian troops won a rare victory over Italian colonial forces, forced the resignation of the veteran statesman Francesco Crispi.

lowing the Emperor's instructions!' So he sent us the painting…one polite gesture deserves another…

"What shall we send him? Well, Monsieur, he's made it known—I have thus from my relative—that he would be happy to have…what? I'll give you a thousand guesses…the academic palm! Not the red ribbon, which is reminiscent of blood—no, the violet ribbon, the emblem of art and literature, the symbol of peaceful works. That'll cause a sensation, don't you think? The presentation of the palm will give way to a fête, and who knows? Who knows…?"

I agree, and then I close my eyes and pretend to go to sleep. Vexed, my neighbor moves away, and soon sleep takes hold of me. The visit of the customs officer wakes me up.

Monsieur Estivoque doesn't bear any grudge. "We'll soon be home," he says. "So long as there isn't too much trouble awaiting us! People are doing everything they can to discourage Commerce and the Economy. Hold on, Monsieur, since it's a long time since you left, perhaps you aren't up to date with one infamous invention. They call it progressive income tax. Have you heard of it?"

"No."

"You're going to hear some bad news, then! From 10,000 francs, they take 1.25%, from 20,000, 2%, from 50,000, 3.25%—with a ceiling that reaches 5%. Terrible, eh?"

"Terrible!"

"And what right do they have to impose what I call an enterprise of ruination and feudalism? What right? Fortunately, we're going to protest. I've drafted a circular. I'll be sure to send you a copy. Might I ask your name and address?"

"Hippolyte Durand, 7, Rue des Lavandières, Sainte Opportune."

Fortunately, another traveler appears. Auguste Estivoque has met him before: "On the Basle train, last winter. You remember—we were held up by snow for three quarters of an hour."

The newcomer is loquacious. I am left in my corner…

I can establish a plan of action.

The address first. In 1896, we were living in the Rue des Archives. I'm not sure of the number, but I can easily find the house again, between a trunk-maker's shop and that of a grocer and pastrymaker. A little further away is the Husseaume bookshop, kept by two hunchbacks, father and son—hunchbacks of giant size, long thin gorillas. One could hire new books from them at ten centimes a day; that's how I learned to read quickly. It required a deposit of three francs. We were so poor that I had to get those three francs back, at my father's insistence. "Very well," said Husseaume the son, who had wrinkled lips in a bony, apoplectic face, "but we won't lend you any more books."

"We'll see—we'll come to some arrangement," said the father, who felt sympathetic toward me because I sometimes borrowed poets that the other customers didn't want—and as I left, he whispered: "Come back, and don't pay any attention to Emile. He's bad-tempered!"

I was ten then; we were to remain in the Rue des Archives for 11 more years. It was there that I felt my first impressions, so profound, that were to make of me the artist that I was unable to remain…

My father, Camille Portereau, was the senior employee of an important drapery wholesalers: Forgeix and

Levacourt. He had started there as a petty clerk and won his modest promotions by hard work, humility and love. In fact, he loved everything about that enterprise, to the prosperity of which he had contributed without benefiting. He was given—"Don't ever complain, it's your marshal's baton," Monsieur Forgeix had specified—400 francs a month, doubled as a Christmas box. At stock-taking, after a week of working all hours, he received some small object as a bonus—a facsimile tie-pin, a napkin-ring, or a wallet with silver initials—all of which he kept in a glass case, as if they were relics.

He loved that gloomy ground-floor, which reeked of flannel, and I think that everywhere else, even at home, he felt out of place. Sometimes, he took us there, at times when there was no one in the shop or the offices. Proudly, he showed us the little well-organized table at which he worked. "Next to the window, you'll notice; I had to wait 15 years, for Bernaque's death, to get my place next to the window." He also loved Monsieur Forgeix, a fat man who oscillated between digestion and indigestion, and who was never comfortable. My father trembled before him, and when he muttered "Lousy weather today!" his employee would signify by his heart-broken expression: "I swear to you, Monsieur, that it isn't my fault!"

He loved even Monsieur Levacourt more, if that were possible, but with a more distant and respectful love, like that of a milkmaid for the local squire. It was said that Monsieur Levacourt was worth more than 20 million. While Monsieur Forgeix neglected himself, preferring loose-fitting clothing, visiting restaurants and going in for base debauchery, Monsieur Levacourt dressed well, frequented racecourses and displayed a premeditated elegance: check trousers, polished boots, embroidered morning-coats, transparent waistcoats and crimson satin shirt-fronts pinned with a large pearl. He only came to the office *en passant*, to collect money or scribble a few signatures, pulling faces like a man over-worked. He never reproached anyone. He even offered an occasional cigar, which my father smoked with ecstatic sensuality. "Monsieur Levacourt gave it to me. He has them specially made in Havana…"

As is often the case, my father, humble and content with everything at Forgeix and Levacourt's, took his revenge in his own house, where he assumed the role of tyrant—a tyrant in slippers, but a tyrant. He expected to be obeyed in his home as he was obedient himself outside it, and he set out to enslave us, in his own interests.

How could that man, imbued with the sternest principles, of whom my mother often said "Camille has everything that a magistrate has—the bearing and the gaze that pierces lies"—a man scrupulous to the point of childishness, who spent a sleepless night for an error in his calculations of ten centimes, ever have come to dishonor himself?

Messieurs Forgeix and Levacourt considered that my father, having been promoted from messenger boy to senior clerk, had been rewarded with an advancement superior to his merits. They watched him grow old with a disapproving eye: an old dog to whom his masters had to "throw a bone," as the English say. He had not shown, in the course of his 30 years of good and loyal service, any worthwhile initiative. Those individuals did not appreciate boundless devotion and reckless gratitude—all the sentiments to which they were obliged to have recourse when they were constrained to search in him for the ultimate resource.

In fact, in the course of their operations, which were not crystal clear, they were led—Monsieur Levacourt by virtue of carelessness and Monsieur Forgeix by virtue of cupidity—to commit one of those stupid errors whose discovery is inevitable. The joke went too far, since the law was aroused and resolved to demand explanations of them. Having been warned, my father's employers ordered him into their office. It was Monsieur Levacourt himself, with his fine check trousers, his satin shirt and his slender side-whiskers in the fashion of 1875, who plucked my father from his table, took him by the arm and led him into the sanctuary of the office, the door of which he carefully closed. It was a matter of finding a guilty party for the law, which would demand no more, but had to have a respondent. Monsieur Forgeix, distraught and sobbing, threw himself at my father's knees and begged him to save the company by taking the blame for the swindle.

Monsieur Levacourt put things in perspective: "These petty infringements go on all the time. I inherited the tradition at birth, if I might put it thus. But we have enemies, my dear Portereau. What they want to get hold of is the company, our Company. Don't think about us— who have, I confess, been imprudent—think about the Company. That's enough of the sentimental part, and I'm sure that it has touched you—let's talk business. Sign these papers, some of which, I won't hide it from you, are antedated—although that will remain between us, Forgeix and I give you our word of honor on that. There will be a trial. You'll be defended by the best advocate in Paris; but whatever happens, once the little affair is settled—and there's every chance that there'll be a dismissal—we'll pay you 400,000 francs. We'll give you an undertaking in writing. We'll pay you

400,000 francs and we'll burn the contract. Afterwards, who'll be retiring to the country, taking up fishing, opening up an ample career for his son and providing his daughter with a nice dowry? Our friend Portereau—for, henceforth, you're no longer our employee—we're friends."

"An entire life of honor," stammered my father, "and I'm going to leave my children a soiled name…"

"Well," Forgeix replied, "if you're going to strike melodramatic poses, good night!"

"We'll shut up shop!" threatened Monsieur Levacourt.

"But it's prison for me!" my father protested. "Prison!"

"Firstly, nothing is less certain, given your past—and anyway," insinuated Monsieur Levacourt, "what are you risking? You have no social status. You'll have a clear conscience, because you know perfectly well that you're innocent. Isn't that the essential thing?"

"I beg your pardon! If I get involved, I become an accomplice!"

"Another word I don't like—a word for the Ambigu! Come on, say yes—sacrifice yourself for your wife, for your children, and for your employers, and everyone will be happy, thanks to you."

One can imagine the agonies that the poor man endured during the minute of reflection that he was granted. That same evening, he had to tell his wife everything—a confidence that I overheard, in my room, by lending an ear to the murmur, in which there was terror and the pride of playing a role—of becoming, in sum the associate of Messieurs Forgeix and Levacourt…

"You understand, my little Rose," he said to my mother, "what would become of me if the business shut down. Who would want me at my age? And Lucie, who needs to be married off? I signed. I put my signature, for the last time as an honest man, at the bottom of their papers…"

My sister Lucie had come into my room. She caught the end of the confession. I was about to run into the room, crying "Papa, don't do this!" She guessed that, and held me back. "Let it go," she whispered, shrugging her shoulders. "It's too late. Don't get mixed up in it."

The slight sound of muffled sobs was heard. It was our mother who was crying. "Come on, it's not 7 p.m. yet," Lucie proposed, still fearing my intervention, "let's go for a walk before dinner." A curious girl, my sister, three years my junior. She had been a taciturn child. I often compared her to one of those Parisian she-cats that remain on watch for hours on end next to a window, in the vain hope of catching a sparrow flying freely through the air. She remained anxious, nervous and feverish until the moment when she could take it for granted that she was pretty. At 16, she was smitten with a young painter who sometimes called in the evening to take tea and nibble a biscuit, while talking to us about his future triumphs. Lucie would only have that one love in her life. It would go no further than a little furtive hand-holding and a few tearful looks. It was the only sentimental page in a life of bitter struggle. Later, while building her fortune, she would think: "I'm not merely a woman of numbers, since I had, at 16, a frustrated passion…" I should add that, rejected by his idol, the painter broke his brushes and left the country in search of some precious metal or other in a land where he died very young. Lucie, in 1896, estimated at 100,000 francs the dowry that would permit her to enter into marriage, and was waiting for the chosen one, François-Alexandre Piou-lette, to become famous or change profession.

The catastrophe occurred in 1897. I would therefore arrive at in time to prevent its occurrence. Thus, inter-ventions that appear supernatural to us might have taken place by mysterious interplanetary exchanges…

To resume the dolorous history of the Portereau family, my father warned us one evening that unforeseen events were about to modify our existence and he begged us not to try to understand them and not to judge him. At that time I had no well-defined profession. I served as secretary to a financier specializing in the con-stitution of societies and the organization of industrial trusts, who confided to me, more or less, the tasks of an office boy. I resolved to leave him. We remained with our mother. In a few weeks she had aged terribly. She still tried to smile at us, to make the customary gestures of daily life, but her poor mouth trembled. One name remains in my memory—that of the great advocate to which Messieurs Forgeix and Levacourt had entrusted the job of defending their employee. Maître Corajoux remained, outside the courtroom, resolutely silent. We assumed that he was very good…

One day, my mother returned home alone and kissed us sadly. My father had been sentenced to a year in prison. "You'll know the whole truth later," she told us. "Continue to love and respect your father. He's a vic-tim."

The trial had taken place in the month of August. It attracted little attention and the newspapers covered it in a few lines. We had, as Monsieur Levacourt had ob-served, no social status. The few friends and relatives that we saw occasionally commiserated with us and dis-appeared. We had to move house. My mother chose a little house in an obscure street in Levallois, flanked by a 400-meter garden. It was there that a year later, to the day, Messieurs Forgeix and Levacourt brought the promised sum, in banknotes. They did not pay too dear. My father was nothing but a wreck. His clothes, which retained the melancholy appearance of a prison uniform, hung loosely about him. He and my mother only went out in the evening, for a short walk in a working-class quarter where they were sure of not meeting anyone they knew. My father retained one hope—that of recovering his place, of sitting down again at his table, next to the window, amid the odor of flannel. Messieurs Forgeix and Levacourt refused. "Damn it, my dear friend—you can live on your income now!"

One might suppose that those gentlemen, having got out of trouble, would have reverted to an elementary prudence. On the contrary; impunity emboldened them. Monsieur Forgeix entered into shady deals. Monsieur Levacourt indulged in a few regrettable pranks. Six months later, they were ruined. In that interval, my father was advised of the death of a great-aunt who had left him her entire fortune, three investment properties in Paris, a château in Saône-et-Loire and significant collections of medals and old paintings. His first concern was to reimburse Messieurs Forgeix and Levacourt, who welcomed that unexpected repayment like manna in the desert. The linen and drapery business—the business of which I had heard so much talk during my childhood—closed its doors.

My sister, brought to despair by the sadness of our surroundings—my father had refused to leave Levallois and the gloomy lodge in which we had taken refuge—married the first rich imbecile who came along, an exceedingly rich orphan introduced by one of his friends.

She left him after a year of discord to establish an even more considerable material situation, thanks to a businessman from Milwaukee, who took her away after her divorce.

My parents had rented me a charming bachelor pad in the Boulevard Malesherbes, and assured me of a good income on condition that I never sought to work. They feared that the opprobrium attacked to the name of Portereau might rebound upon me in society.

I was sensitive, but I still feel remorse at not having surrounded both of them with affection and sympathy. Drunk with liberty and glutted with money, I never went back without apprehension to that gloomy, meanly-furnished flowerless dwelling, where a double grief was displayed. I dined there two or three times a week. At 10 p.m., I was liberated by a "Leave us now; go amuse yourself." I protested, for form's sake, and left.

One evening, I heard my father, who thought I had gone although I was still in the antechamber, sigh: "He's lucky! He's an elector! He can hold his head up!" He imagined that his whole story, already plunged into the anonymity of the past, was known to everyone. In Levallois, my parents' reclusiveness was attributed to pious sentiments, an unforgettable mourning or one of those semi-ruinations that transforms bourgeois opulence into meager retreat.

My parents died in 1900, within a few weeks of one another. When I was alone, I regretted never having shared a complete explanation with them—one of those heart-rending and beneficent scenes that wash away human misery in tears. The division of the succession brought about a definitive split with my sister. Those formalities having been regulated, entering into possession of a massive fortune, hardened by everything I had seen or endured—not loving one woman, or even women in general, but woman in the abstract—concerned with comfort, open to matters of intellect, expecting nothing from life but which it provided so easily, I imagined that, for me, everything was beginning...

In fact, everything had finished.

VI.

Paris! The Paris of 1896, which smells of horse manure and faded lilacs. I have the sensation of entering a City of the Dead. These people bustling, jostling one another, running in all directions, knowing in the meantime that they are destined to die…they know it, but they do not believe it. I used to have the same impression at the theater: spectators weeping or laughing at the ridicule or anguish evoked, as if they were not exposed to such things themselves. Then I thought: "How many among the will have disappeared tomorrow? Which of these unconscious individuals are already marked by Destiny?"

That baby in the arms of its nurse will be 18 years old in 1914…

The old coachman that my porter has chosen, doubtless because he has the most worn-out horse, the ruddiest face and the most evil disposition, is astonished that I am not waiting for heavier luggage. "You can see that I have a roof-rack. It's for loading trunks. I've been waiting for three hours—of all the cursed luck!"

His sentiment is endorsed by a man in rags—the bag-man who runs after cabs in order to carry the trunks into houses, thus earning ten *sous*. "It oughtn't to be allowed!" he groans.

My porter, however, reassured by his tip, tries to convince the coachman. He affirms that I'm a good bourgeois, generous to the poor. These people are in no hurry; I intervene: "Yes or no? Make up your mind."

"First, where are you going?"

I give the approximate address of a hotel in the Rue Richer. The Rue Richer is to the Automedon's liking. He picks up his reins. The horse pulls away and I collapse on to an exceedingly hard banquette. Obsolete cabs! Cabs of my youth! This one is upholstered in what was once blue velvet. The dolorous trot of the wretched beast that is pulling me makes me feel ill...

The journey will be interminable. I once made up a story—a fairy tale—for I never ceased to read and imagine such things. A man, on the point of crushing a mayfly, suddenly stops out of respect for life and lets the insect fly away—and the insect rewards him by giving him its own notion of time, thus lengthening the existence of it benefactor immeasurably. What is a minute for us lasts six months for a mayfly, born at dawn and dying during the night. I thought about my hero, and estimated that the cab ride from the Gare de l'Est to the Rue Richer would take several years. I tried to interest myself in the streets. What emotion I would feel if I recognized a passer-by! The gentlemen ornamented by proud moustaches, the ladies with their ugly and complicated costumes seem to me to be playing a retrospective scene in a Revue in which I represent the Present, amid caricaturish shades...

If I were listening to my heart, I would hurry right away to the Rue des Archives, but I do not want to appear before my family until I was washed and shaved—in short, "at my best." I plan to introduce myself at first as an unknown relative. It is necessary not to give them the impression of a tiresome person who might eventually want to borrow money...

I knock on the window.

"Do you want me to stop?" grumbles the apoplectic driver.

"Yes."

"I warn you that it'll be the same tariff as moving."

"Of course."

He tugs brutally on the reins; the nag stumbles, but reestablishes its tremulous equilibrium by some miracle.

"Eh! I'll be over there!" cries the coachman. "I'll need a deposit."

Obviously, I do not inspire confidence. That fortifies me in my resolution to prepare for my entrance in the Rue des Archives. I give him the deposit and I go into a celebrated confectioner's shop. There, I choose one of those enormous boxes of chocolates that were then put in the window display, in the ever-unrealized hope of achieving a strange ostentation. On satin of the most false color, the box bears a painting depicting a couple of kittens playing with a ball of string. I point it out to the shop-girl. "That's a work of art, and signed," she remarks. "Full, it costs 500 francs."

I dispense that sum, and the shop-girl takes a good quarter of an hour to align the chocolates in the box.

The coachman opens the door. "Are you finished yet?" he asks, severely.

Finally, I carry away the package, duly done up with gold thread and wrapped. In the carriage, I calculate that my meager capital is beginning to dwindle—but are not all financial possibilities open to me, in this naïve world to which I am bringing Progress?

I could not find the hotel where I had often accommodated provincial relatives. I left the cab after having tipped the driver so lavishly that, thinking that I had made a mistake and fearing that I would call him back, he whipped his horse cruelly, which departed this time at a gallop.

I went into a hotel of modest appearance. The manager looked me up and down without enthusiasm, enquired about my luggage and, having been informed, assigned me a cupboard under the eaves for the price of four francs a day. I filled out the registration form in the name of André Portereau, from Canada.

"Canada!" the manager declared suspiciously. "That's not across the street."

I informed him of my intention to take a bath.

"Perhaps that's the fashion over there, in hotels!" the manager insinuated, with sharp irony. "Here, one goes to the establishment that is a few steps away, where you'll find all that you need, in the way of soap and towels. My wife and I used to go there, when we were young."

I cast an eye over the closet that had been allotted to me: a camp-bed, a washstand with a doll's basin, a white wood table, a caved-in chair. Afterwards, I was able to take a bath, whose preparation only required half an hour. "We're full," the attendant said, by way of excuse. "Tomorrow's a holiday!" I finally plunged myself into hot water, where I remained for a long time, in order to calm my impatience. Besides, as the critical moment approached, I had an obscure desire to put it off. I would not go to the Rue des Archives until meal-time, when I would find my dear family together. How could I support such a strong emotion without weakening?

While I dress carefully, having returned to my hovel, nibbling a one-*sou* croissant dipped in a miserly cup of coffee, I examine myself. This oval mirror is blurred, but inexorable. The Maxime Portereau of 1935 inevitably resembles the Maxime Portereau of 1896. He had a moustache, whereas I am clean-shaven; what remains of my hair, once abundant and the warmest shade of blond, is almost entirely white, and one could count the hairs individually—but the nose and the eyes are the same, as are the height and the voice. I can already hear my mother's cry of surprised: "How he resembles Maxime!" I shall lie, at first—but what if the melodramas of the Boulevard du Crime[5] call "the voice of the blood" is determined to speak? What if my mother, who is only thirty-eight years old, recognizes her child in the aged visitor, and opens her arms to me? I shall not hide the incredible truth. She will believe me. I will resume, in the company of my double, my place at the hearth where I shall play the role of Providence, from which I shall lift the curses of the future. And later, still young, she will be able to witness her old son, in his dying moments...

Gently, gently... No lyricism; self-composure. In less extraordinary circumstances, I am always forced to struggle against my natural impulsiveness. I succeed in that by being very methodical, by complete submission to a plan established after mature reflection. The system has always worked. In those complicated affairs from which I emerged victorious, I began with a profound meditation. I examined the various possible outcomes, favorable and unfavorable. Finally, I arrived fully-equipped before a surprised interlocutor who had not had the opportunity to prepare himself. This time, especially, when I would need to commit myself body and soul, I had to proceed with the same circumspection, restraining every impulse under threat of being taken for a lunatic and seeing two male nurses assure me of an eternal re-

---

[5] The Boulevard du Temple, legendary—especially in the old novels of which the narrator is so fond—for its theaters specializing in bloody melodramas, such as the aforementioned Ambigu.

treat in an alienist's resting-place. I still had the memory of the Austrian hell, the ignoble shower, and my neighbors: the sobbing madman and the other, even more unbearable, who laughed at everything and thought himself at the height of bliss…

My street…

The shop run by the two booksellers breathes into my face the familiar odor of stew and rancid old books.

"Can I help you. Monsieur?" Here is Husseaume junior, who will die in 1898 of apoplexy. He flashes me a commercial smile. Shall I say to him: "It's me, little Maxime Portereau, whom you detest. Do you remember? I came to hire the novels of Henry Gréville, Alphonse Karr and Paul de Kock, and I left your shop with my weekly provision of dreams!"

"A notebook and a pencil."

Monsieur Husseaume senior emerges from the shadows. With his hump, his white moustache and his goatee he is a cross between a musketeer and Quasimodo. The unfamiliar customer visibly intrigues him. Perhaps he remembers him from somewhere…

Bitten by curiosity, he asks:" Should we deliver them to your home?"

"No. I'll take them with me."

Disappointment.

I cannot help saying, as I go out: "Bonjour, Messieurs Husseaume!" A grave imprudence.

The two hunchbacks look at one another, amazed. The name Husseaume is not inscribed on the shop. The son makes as if to call me back. They must be following me with their gaze, exchanging bewildered comments. Don't indulge in such childishness again, at all costs…

My house…

What floor? The second? Third? I no longer remember. In the main body of the building, which fronts on to the street, is the concierge's lodge.

"Madame…?"

I was about to say "Madame Juque." She is, as always, stirring perfumed broth in a saucepan. I imagine her as a centenarian; her hair is scarcely graying.

"Close the door—you can see that you're creating a draught."

"Yes, Madame. Monsieur Portereau, if you please?" I have reverted to the humility of my childhood!

"Which one?" Madame Juque demands. "The father or the son?"

"Both."

"They're not here."

"And Madame?"

"Look—back of the courtyard, fourth above the entresol, door on the left."

I try to walk confidently, but my legs tremble.

The stairway, with its patchwork of truffles, pistachios and bacon, in the guise of false marble! The banister, astride which I effected bold descents—the only sport of my youth in those days…

I consult my watch. Three o'clock. Suddenly, panic grips me. I think about *The Monkey's Paw* in which a couple in possession of a fetish can make three wishes. After the second, by means of which they wanted to bring their son back from the dead, the parents hear his familiar greeting, shivering with terror, and use their last wish to send him away without seeing him...above all, without seeing him...[6]

I will be stronger.

I climb the stairs slowly, very slowly, but I go all the way. The landing...

The stain: an insulting graffito scrawled by a discontented tradesman, which we had erased. I forget the heaviness with which the five sets of stairs have just afflicted me. I'm twenty years old again. I'm coming home. I'm no longer afraid. Already, it's as if I'm enveloped by tenderness. Mechanically, I pat my pocket, in order to find my key, given to me on my eighteenth birthday. "Don't abuse it!"

But no...you're still only a stranger. You have to ring the bell, like a stranger. I pull the marrow woven cord, my sister's work. The sound is shrill and nostalgic, as if advertising the fact that I have come from far way...very far away, from another planet...

The muffled sound of voices...

They aren't expecting anyone...

Silence. I ring again. The bell sounds more imperiously, as if it were signifying: "It's me! Look, Mama, me!"

The door opens slightly. The little maid Madeleine, always unkempt, who nursed a secret passion for me and served me as if she were caressing me, with an anxious fervor...

"What is it?" she asks.

---

[6] It is unclear whether or not Duvernois expects his readers to remember that in the famous story by W. W. Jacobs, the parents are reminded by the peculiar sound of their son's approach that he was dismembered in a terrible accident.

"Would you tell Madame that one of her cousins is here."

"One of her…?"

"Cousins."

"Wait a minute!"

She isn't very well-trained; she leaves me on the doorstep. I hear my mother's voice, such a clear voice: "Ask him which cousin?"

"A cousin from Canada."

"Good. Wait."

I cock my ear.

"Cousin Canada," Madeleine announces.

My sister intervenes. "She never understands. It must be Casimir. Show him into the drawing-room."

Scolded for my sin, Madeleine introduces me sullenly into the drawing-room, or the room that we have baptized thus. Here is my sister Lucie's bed-settee, the copper and lapis-lazuli candelabra on the mantelpiece, the imitation-oak chairs upholstered in worn red velvet, the rubber plant in a pot decorated with a cerise ribbon, and, on the side-table in front of the window, my portrait as a schoolboy…

I sit down, my knees apart. Will I be able to pronounce the sentences that I've prepared. I must. I must also hold back the sob that is rising into my throat. Above all, no tears—the indication of mental deficiency, according to the male nurse in Vienna.

Indifferece… Smile…

The door opens…

Mama!

How young she is, and how pretty! The first triumph: I can smile at this delightful mother, who is 38 and doesn't look a day over 30…

"Monsieur?"

I stammer: "My child…"

Astonished, she takes a step back. I start again: "Permit me to address you thus, or as Rose…my age authorizes it. May I introduce myself: André Portereau."

"Sit down, I beg you. I've never heard mention…"

"I'm your cousin—or, rather, the first cousin of Camille, your husband. André Portereau, son of Raymond Portereau, who was exiled at a young age…"

"Indeed…"

"And who never sent news again. I've brought you this box…"

"That's very kind of you."

She unties the package, sees the picture of the kittens playing with the ball of string, and murmurs politely "It's delightful! A charming idea!" She asks me a few questions, which reveal, beneath the most cordial politeness, a certain anxiety. I reply as best I can. I establish the purely imaginary history of Raymond Portereau, grown rich in the fur trade, who never had time to write a letter but who had retained the veneration of the family, piously transmitted to his son.

"Is this the first time you've come to France, Monsieur?"

"Call me André. Yes, Rose, it's the first time."

"You don't have an accent."

"We speak French at home."

"But you speak English as well as French, naturally."

"No. I left Canada a long time ago. I've been traveling…"

"My daughter speaks very good English. Lucie! Lucie!"

And my sister appears. Her black hair, her blue eyes, her cold beauty…

"Madeleine wasn't mistaken. Lucie," my mother says. "Monsieur André Portereau, one of our cousins, who has had the kind inspiration of coming to visit us."

"But how did you know how to find us?" asks Lucie.

"My father, whom I have lost…"

"Oh! Was it long ago?" asks my mother.

"Oh, yes. I'm over 60, you know…"

"One would not think so."

"My father always took an interest in all of you. He was very well-organized. He had a card-index…"

I'm beginning to get confused. Fortunately, these details do not captivate my audience.

"Look at the superb box that our cousin has brought us," says my mother.

At once, Lucie the haughty young woman becomes a little girl. She neglects the work of art painted on the lid, opens the box and bites into a chocolate.

"You must excuse her; she has to go to a musical performance given by one of her former teachers."

Lucie gets up, as if set free, gives me a little curtsy, as one does to old men, and disappears…

"She's adorable," I declare.

"She's genteel."

"You only have one child?"

"No, I also have a son…"

My heart beats faster. "How old is he?"

"19.[7] I hope you'll make his acquaintance soon."

---

[7] This is inconsistent with the birth date given at the beginning of the story and the date of the landing as reported by the civil

"I look forward to it."

"He's something of a prodigy…"

"Ah!"

"One might say that he's multitalented. At the age of six he composed a sonata, like Mozart. He has sculpted statuettes in wax in which an eminent sculptor, now retired, recognized the touch of Carpeaux. The other day, while I was trying to tidy his room, I found models of châteaux—he's also an architect. You must get him to read you his verses. Most of the time he tears them up or burns them. Fortunately, he's not very orderly. I pick up the papers behind his back and keep them. His precocity sometimes frightens us…at ten he wrote an amorous sonnet inspired by some little girl or other, which is a masterpiece…"

I remember the masterpiece in question. It began: *Florine, all of springtime is in your eyes/And I adore you, because you're so wise…*

My smile vexes my mother. "We didn't want to push him too hard when he was small; he frightened us…"

"What career has he chosen?"

"He's too artistic to sell his talents. He thinks seriously about life. For the moment, he's advising a great financier who can't do without him. He intends to establish his material situation first. Child's play, for him! At school, he dashed off his homework in a few minutes, and was always near the top of the class. He never memorized a lesson; he read it once and that was enough. I've kept his end-of-term reports: the headmaster wrote: *a prodigiously gifted pupil…*"

---

servant in Kahlenberg; according to those Maxime should now be four months past his 20th birthday.

The headmaster added: *but deplorably nonchalant.* My mother omits that slight correction. I can no longer restrain myself; I get up and kiss her cheeks.

"What!" she cries. "You're leaving already!"

I had no intention of leaving, but my mother has stood up. She has exhausted all that she has to say about her son—and she finds me too expansive.

"You must come to dinner one evening."

"Gladly."

"Arrange a day with my husband."

"When can I see him?"

"In his office, at Forgeix and Levacourt's, 2 Rue des Jeûners. Tell the young man on the platform at the entrance to ask for him. Don't stand on ceremony, cousin. I'd especially like you to meet Maxime. I'm sure you'll find him interesting…"

"So am I."

"And, especially, don't feel obliged to bring flowers or sweets. You've already spoiled me too much!"

"What do you expect?—it's my reason for being, now. I no longer have anyone else."

"Have you been married?"

"No."

"A bachelor! That's a shame!"

"If I'd ever met a woman like you…"

"Me? I'm full of faults. I've only been able to be a mother."

"That's sufficient."

I kiss her again, this time with a little more insistence than is warranted. My mother pulls away gently. A brief silence. She looks at me. I divine the mute question: *Who are you? What are doing in our life?* I squeeze her hands, her soft hands. I must be pulling a strange face. My mother decides to laugh at it. "A trifle eccentric, our cousin," she will say, this evening.

"Don't forget the address of Camille's office: 2, Rue des Jeûners. You're sure to find him there—he never goes out. Goodbye. I'm delighted to have met you…"

And, after a brief hesitation, she adds an "André". In which I detect an obscure pity for an old man whose ears are no longer caressed by his forename…

I leave…

And I suddenly feel cold, as if I had just been sent away…

VII.

As I have already noted, my father never let us come to see him in his office during working hours. Before the catastrophe, and even afterwards, he inspired me with a respectful dread, retained from childhood, in which he figured, for my sister and me, as the supreme judge handing down implacable sentences. In order not to appear too old in the eyes of Messieurs Forgeix and Levacourt, he dyed his hair, but the hairdresser to whom he entrusted himself employed a cheap dye that spread a tint of black lead over the hair and marbled the scalp with brown patches. He was a little man, taciturn and solemn, whom Mama had married without love, but to whom she remained grateful for having given her an exceptional progeniture: a dazzling daughter and a son of genius.

As a child, I conceived the most flattering opinion of the man who had given me the light of day. I saw him plunged in books and disdainful of our frivolous distractions. Later on, I observed that the books were not lofty philosophy, but emanated from Vast-Ricouard, Mayne Reid and other armchair voyagers.[8] He was totally un-

---

[8] Raoul Vast (1850-1889) and Gustave Ricouard (1853-1887) enjoyed a meteoric collaborative career in the early 1880s, producing several highly successful novels and plays as Vast-Ricouard before both dying young. The Irish-American author Mayne Reid (1818-1883) enjoyed a similar temporary success in the 1850s and 1860s, enjoying—like several other writers of adventure stories set in America—a particular popularity in France.

known to me. Careful of respectability, he only ever appeared before us clad in his morning-suit and austerity. He reigned over the three children of his household—his son, his daughter and his wife—saying "my little Rose" as he said "my little Lucie" or "my little Maxime." He intended to be respected and he had complained of me, my mother told me, "That boy doesn't respect me," when I was not yet a year old. I believe that he had never nurtured any other ambition than to be employed at Forgeix and Levacourt's. To maintain a superiority over his colleagues, he was never absent. He was the man who never took vacations. He sent us to the seaside for a few days and took advantage of them to carry out reorganizations in the office that permitted the busy season to be confronted with confidence. He might have been afraid of plunging us into poverty by disappearing, but he counted on the good will of Messieurs Forgeix and Levacourt...

I asked for him at the entrance. An employee who was surreptitiously smoking a cigarette, shielded in his hand, blew out his smoke under the table and said, boorishly: "You'll find him in the hall."

I could, indeed, see my father, who was showing a new boy the art of placing an item of drapery correctly in a showcase.

"I've got it!" retorted the new boy, an urchin with an insolent expression, sleeves that were too short and red hands. "That's ten times you've told me the same thing! I'm not thick..."

"I'll thank you to speak to me in a different tone!" exclaimed my father. "We don't use slang here."

I present myself. "Monsieur Camille Portereau?"

"Indeed. How can I help you?"

"I'm one of your cousins: André Portereau, the son of Raymond Portereau."

"Are you looking for a position?"

"Not at all. I've just come from your home. Rose told me where to find you, and as I was eager to shake your hand…"

"My wife should not have done that," my poor father muttered. "I can't receive anyone here. I regret…we're snowed under with work."

"Portereau!" cut in a dry voice, "When will you have terminated this personal conversation?"

I turned round. I was face to face with Monsieur Forgeix, one of the men responsible for all our future misfortunes: an obese and slovenly Monsieur Forgeix, who was chewing a cigar furiously, as if he had a desire to spit in my face.

I had raised my hat. I lowered it again, to my father's terror.

"It's not a matter of personal conversation," I said. "I came to see your samples with a view to placing an order, but I see that I've come at a bad time, and I'll go."

"Wait," begged Monsieur Forgeix, mollified. "You don't have to explain, damn it. Why are you addressing yourself to an employee? I'm here. Come into my office."

The sight of the enemy did me good. I went into the office.

"My associate is not here," Monsieur Forgeix told me. "He never is. He goes on the spree in the afternoon, because his doctor has instructed him not to go to be too late. I'm stuck here, with Portereau, who's completely gaga…"

"I'm his cousin," I objected, "and I believed that he has shown you appreciable marks of devotion."

"But has he sold any cloth? That's the question! Not a centimeter!"

"I shall fill that lacuna."

"You're a buyer?"

"Perhaps."

"To whom do I have the honor of speaking?"

"André Portereau."

"You know that we don't sell retail?"

"I know."

I know from personal experience that there is a particular way of talking to men of Forgeix's stripe—a curt tone that impresses them. I dazzled him with the prospect of establishing a department store in Paris that would sell all kinds of items at a uniquely low price.

"We already have that for men's hats."

"That's nothing; I shall extend the idea to a range of merchandise, including food."

"You're probably in search of capital?" Forgeix sniggered.

"No, it will be provided by three banks and myself. I don't need money or credit. I pay *cash*."[9]

"Pardon?"

"Ready money—but I require a discount, which I'll agree with you later. Show me your samples…"

I had him at my mercy. He took a bottle of simulated Cognac out of a safe and invited me to appreciate the vitriol. I had kept my hat on my head, which succeeded in convincing him that I was not a beggar. When the conversation was over, he wanted to take me to a café: "You'll have a glass of beer, informally…"

---

[9] This word is rendered in English in the original, which is why the narrator then has to translate it for Forgeix's benefit.

Before leaving, I spotted my father bent over his table. "Camille," I said, "we haven't had a chance to chat…"

"Come to the café with us, old man," Monsieur Forgeix conceded.

"I have to make up the C.B.X. account for the messenger…but André, if you would like to give me the pleasure of dining at the house on…let's see…today's Monday—shall we say Thursday?"

"Soup and beef?" asked Monsieur Forgeix, jovially. "If there's soup and beef, I'll come myself."

"Oh, Monsieur Forgeix," murmured my father, dazzled.

"Agreed. We'll both be there at 8 p.m." And he concluded, as he drew me away: "He's a good chap—fundamentally a nonentity, but a good chap. His wife and kids must think that he's in his prime rather than past it!"

It's 7 p.m. I've left Forgeix half-asleep on a pile of saucers. He likes me, visibly. He thinks that I've adopted a strange way of doing business, which seems to him to be excellent. I want to talk to him about my father, to convince him the he will henceforth have in me a friend and protector, and that his honor is as precious to me as my own—but this doesn't seem to be the right time. Monsieur Forgeix drank a lot and told me dirty jokes, after which he became sentimental. He has lady friends, whom he likes plump and amiable, in a few nearby establishments. "They call me Toto…I'm famous under the name of Toto in those places!" He was completely won over when I paid the bill.

Now I'm outside, resuming my search. I rarely dined at home in this period. I spent my scant pocket money at a little restaurant in the Rue Le Peletier, which my comrades frequented.

Here they come…Fournier, killed in 1915, a pale adolescent, timid and charming, who wants to go into the theater and, working all day, takes lessons in the evening from an old actor at the Association Philotechnique; Hochetain, a teacher at an institution for deaf-mutes; Gomieux, a notary's clerk.

"Pardon me, gentleman, is Maxime Portereau coming this evening?"

"We don't know," Gomieux replies. "He usually turns up around this time. There's a lady waiting for him…"

The lady who is waiting for him in Choute. I recognize her. She spent a year waiting for me. There she is, innocent and resigned, in her poor little bonnet. "Oh," she murmurs, "I'll be surprised if he doesn't come."

I sit down next to her. My little mistress, tender and faithful…perhaps the only one. I left her for the benefit of so many others who weren't worth as much! I tell her my story: an old cousin come from abroad. She pretends to listen to me and watches the clock, while consuming a horrible bowl of soup with an industrial odor, into which she has crumbled a bread roll.

"What will you have now, Mademoiselle?"

"Oh! Nothing, thank you, Monsieur. I'm waiting for Maxime."

Maxime won't come. As I start on my dessert, Hochetain beckons to me. I get up and rejoin him. He whispers in my ear: "Don't tell the girl, but at 9 p.m., he'll definitely be at the Moulin Rouge."

I did, indeed, often go to the Moulin Rouge, having obtained my introduction there thanks to Gomieux, in the capacity of a theatrical messenger, on an intermittent daily basis.

Choute has given up hope. I fail to pay the bill for her soup. "Maxime wouldn't like it. Thank you, Monsieur, for the kind thought." With a heart-rending smile she says to the waiter: "That will be all for this evening, Emile; I'm not hungry." She isn't hungry. I know where she's going, to an attic in the Rue des Marais. There she knits little dresses and makes braid. She makes three francs a day and is proud of not taking a *sou* from anyone. It's necessary to look at her attentively for some time to find her pretty.

Memories! Our first rendezvous, in a suburban bar. The rain. The booth where we held one another tightly, and her prayer: "You won't make me too unhappy?" She could foresee…

The Moulin Rouge. Cadaverous women eyeing up potential clients with a sort of hatred. One of them, drunk, is heaping copious insults on a former companion, now settled down, who is taking her ease in the enclosure reserved for important customers: "Just because you have a pearly dress and a feathery hat…but we know you…you're Fanny! What about Mother Louise, eh? You didn't put on airs when you were with Mother Louise, did you?"

Challenged, the other tries to laugh: "She's confusing me with someone else. It's too funny!" And she takes as her witnesses the man who are accompanying her and wish they were somewhere else.

Somber pleasures. A Toulouse-Lautrec: the naturalist quadrille, applauded by the amateurs; a hieratic dance. Robust thighs, thick ankles, vulgar legs earnestly raised in a medley of fake lace petticoats. In the garden, women go by, mounted on donkeys, forcing themselves to be cheerful...

I search...

And finally, I find...

That feverish young man with his back against a pillar, who seems to be on the lookout—that's me!

I stop. What drama might be upsetting me at this moment? Abruptly, the memories flood back in profusion. Everything becomes clear...

I was in love with Fanny—the same one that the streetwalker was insulting. And Fanny was drinking with rich young men—fops, as they say. "And so handsome, too!" my mother had declared. I don't find myself handsome. I feel neither keen excitement nor ardent pity. I force myself to repeat: "That's you! That's your youth." I can't persuade myself...

I remember this evening. I know that, after that long wait, I precipitated myself on to the platform, shouting, "Come on, that's enough! Are you coming?" amid the indignant protests of the fops—and Fanny said: "What more does he want from me." A scandal, my visiting card thrown in the face of the one who seemed to me to be protecting the chosen one most particularly. The intervention of a *maître d'hôtel*. "You have no business here—get out immediately!" And as the fops made themselves scarce, because things were turning ugly, I left with the spoils of war, escorting Fanny, regal and subjugated, so beautiful in her red dress with the pearly train, white with fear beneath her make-up.

I shall prevent that grotesque scene.

"Are you Maxime Portereau?"

"Yes."

"I'm your cousin André."

"Ah! I know...my mother told me..."

"I'm happy to see you."

"Me too! How did you recognize me?"

"Your portrait on the side-table…and there's a family resemblance, isn't there?"

"Perhaps…"

"May I get you something?"

"No thank you. I'm waiting for someone."

"Here?"

"Here? We're dining together on Thursday, aren't we?"

"I hoped to find you in the Rue Le Peletier."

"I don't go there anymore."

"I had a chat with your little friend, Choute. She's delightful."

"She's a nice girl…" Maxime-Félix Portereau replies to his double distractedly. He only has eyes for Fanny. He catches sight of her. It pains him to see her being so familiar with those people—but that pain scarcely touches me.

"Come on," I say. "I can see what's going on. At the risk of annoying you, I won't let you go. Let's sit down—and you can open your heart to me. I was once young, like you. We're related. Let's be friends."

"Certainly!"

I would seal the friendship with an offer of 20 louis, but I know that the very idea of a loan would fill me with horror. "Let's sit down," I propose.

He prefers to remain standing against the column, watching Fanny. When serious, she is almost ugly, but laughter transforms her; she has a splendid jaw—the jaw of a young wild beast-and her eyes, dull until then, take on a marvelous gleam. When she wants to be seductive, she laughs. Tonight, she is laughing a great deal.

"Is that her?"

"Yes."

Maxime-Félix Portereau, who is very well-dressed for the occasion, with a top hat and yellow gloves, finally turns away and draws up a chair next to my armchair. Then I hear an idiotic hymn of praise to that woman, vehemently pronounced. She is not what vain people think. Once, she was married and her ex-husband, a Brazilian, gives her an income that ensures her independence. Only, she has been so unhappy—"He hit her in front of their 35 servants"—that she is jealous of her liberty. Although madly in love—and Maxime is modestly implying "madly in love with me"—she intends to remain free. "And this evening, what she's doing is solely to test me, to establish her independence...." But in the intimacy of the night, she is as fearful as a little girl, she begs forgiveness, she swears that she will never do it again, that she is scornful of the imbeciles with whom she pretends to amuse herself. She is, according to Maxime-Félix, the most sensitive and generous creature. She adores Delmet's ballads and always has flowers in her window, like the Lady of the Camellias.[10] Her health is precarious too...

I have a strong desire to interrupt. I know all this. But a friend is, first and foremost, a pair of ears. I need to conquer the friendship of my young double. Nothing easier—it is enough to listen and approve, to avoid saying, for instance: "Fanny is a crane and you're a silly

---

[10] Paul Delmet (1862-1904) was a famous cabaret singer and composer, noted for his *romances* [sentimental ballads]. *La Dame aux camelias* (1848) is a tragic romance by Alexandre Dumas *fils*, enormously popular in its day, about a high-class whore doomed by her love for a starry-eyed young man and tuberculosis.

goose." I'll save that for later. I hope that, when the chapter is exhausted, we'll pass on to other topics of conversation. All the same, at that age, I had higher desires, more noble aspirations. I wasn't only this sort of animal, obsessed with his desire and ravaged with jealousy....

I try to tear myself away from my obsession. No, I try to tear Maxime away. I divine that I no longer have anything in common with him. I lean over my youth, and I find another person. On politics and literature, he emits a few curt and ill-founded opinions, which exasperate me. And that self-confidence! That naivety! That fatuity! What he thinks is doubtless worth more than what he says. He's thinking of nothing but Fanny, and he's raving...

Suddenly, he can no longer hold still. "Will you excuse me? One minute..."

And the scene—the scene that I could not prevent—unfolds again. I hear a noise, the squeals of frightened women. I see Maxime, his cane raised, with the arm of a *maître d'hôtel* around his body. I hear: "Come on, that's enough! Are you coming!" The intervention of a policeman. "I have his name—he'll have to be barred, the hooligan!" And I follow the couple: Maxime victorious, still trembling with wrath; Fanny furious, but tamed. I catch up with them. I share the reprobation that accompanies them to the exit, the hoots of the streetwalkers, desirous of keeping in the good graces of the administration. I mention a little supper. Maxime declines; Fanny hastens to accept. We go into a nearby café.

"Go wash your hands, my darling," Fanny advises.

In the struggle with the *maître d'hôtel*, Maxime has skinned his knuckles. He hesitates momentarily, then sets off for the washroom.

"He's nice little fellow," Fanny whispers to me, "but he doesn't know what's what."

"I expect you feed him a load of claptrap!"

"He needs it! He demands it! He's a child, to whom it's necessary to tell stories to settle him down. Certainly, it'd be better if he left me alone, but he paces up and down in front of my door for hours. Then I open up. I'm a hussy, but I'm not wicked."

"Do you love him?"

Again that cruel, resplendent laughter. "For that, he'd have to come back when he's lived a little. You ought to advise him to stay calm. You know, Monsieur, one can hardly believe that he works. He doesn't do anything. He runs to me afterwards. He writes to me three times a day, eight-page letters of which I don't understand a word." She gives me a velvety wink. "What I'd like is a master, a man who knows his mind. These children always need rocking, consoling, even when one has a headache. One becomes, as they say—not me, mind—their nurse. While a man of your sort…"

My word, Fanny's giving me the eye!

A little later, when all three of us are installed, Maxime proud of his wounds and his conquest, she plays footsie with me. She declares that she's never been so happy. Obscurely, she has realized a troilistic feminine dream; she divines, in addition to the presence of an ardent and awkward desire, that of a lukewarm protection. We add up to a single lover who combines all the physical and mental qualities, to whom she can be alternately mother and child. That troubles me. For two pins I'd respond to the pressure of her knee, the appeal of her foot. I breathe in Fanny's perfume. It intoxicates me. It still pleases me.

92

Maxime gulps down a bowl of onion soup and devours several slices of almost-raw roast beef. It's the time when the music becomes languorous and the customers become poetic. Maxime's appetite sickens Fanny. She pushes away her full plate. She drinks, looking at me incessantly—and the young lover begins to get anxious. He wants to shine, He talks non-stop. He recounts the ups and downs of three or four duels, one to the death, and Fanny shrugs her shoulders at the lies. Young men pass by, who smile at her. Maxime gets exasperated. "What if I were to give them a few slaps, eh?" She calms him down by stroking his hand, and as she intends to share herself, she strokes my hand at the same time. Maxime abruptly withdraws his own.

It's time for me to go. I pay…

"When will we see you again?" Fanny asks.

"Soon."

"Swear?"

"Promise."

Maxime takes his leave of me gladly. "Until Thursday," he says.

"Until Thursday." I add: "Consider me as your other self!"

"Thanks!"

I go back to the Rue Richer on foot. I feel disillusioned; I would rather think that I were better looking; I would rather think that I were more intelligent; I would rather think I were better all round…

VIII.

I need money—lots of money—in order to become master of all these destinies. I therefore decide to go and see my uncle and godfather Félix-Amédée Portereau.[11] He is very rich, miserly, and ferociously greedy. I know that he is annoyed with my family, following a discussion of which I was the topic.

"You fawn over that boy," my uncle declared, "and you encourage his idleness. Put him to work seriously. Let him study law, for example. It's hindered me a great deal not to have made such a study. If he's counting on my money to play the dandy, he's mistaken! Not a *sou*! He shan't have a *sou*!"

"Has he asked you for anything?" my father asked.

"No,"

"Then you're annoying us. Take your advice elsewhere."

"I'll take you at your word!"

Thus, I was deprived of the modest obligatory lottery ticket that my godfather sent me every January the first, and which I immediately sold. "If you win a prize, I'll let you know—I've written down your number," he told me. Fortunately, he never had to let me know. Félix-Amédée had lived to the most extreme limit, since he had died in 1925, almost a centenarian. He had various business interests—robbing inventors, introducing him-

---

[11] The reader might remember, although the author apparently does not, that the narrator was supposedly named Maxime after his godfather, not Félix, only acquiring the latter name because it was hoped that he might be happy.

94

self into failing business, into which he breathed a semblance of life before selling them on at a tidy profit to benevolent amateurs, whose race is inexhaustible—but his favorite sin remained usury, in which he had made his brilliant debut. He came back to it as to a mistress. Nothing seemed to him more delightful than the son of a family who came to him bound hand and foot, with urgent debts and solid guarantees. The more credulous and helpless he found him, the more he pampered him. For two pins, he would have kissed him. He said to him: "Don't worry about it anymore, trust Papa Portereau." He knew how to put on a paternal unctuousness that won him, as well as a monstrous percentage, the gratitude of his victims. He called them his chickens. He considered them with the expertise of a cook plucking a bird, meditating on the tasty meal he would make of them…

This shark, to whom innumerable ruinations and bankruptcies were due, had a flash of conscience before yielding his soul. That ignoble existence ended with a fine testament that enriched the good causes to which Félix-Amédée, while alive, would have refused a centime. I had my share, in a paragraph that resembled a curse.

In 1896, from 10 a.m. until noon, my godfather lurked in an office where he spread out his spider's web, waiting for the poor flies that would be caught in it. His unfortunate clients lines up on hard benches, in a waiting-room in which a Boulle-style clock in very bad taste but enormous, beat out the seconds noisily, as if to apprise those fantasists of the price of time. The office was the only furnished room in a vast house in a damp street in Neuilly. According to his own expression, Félix-Amédée had bought the house for a mouthful of bread, thus sowing discord among a band of heirs who were never reconciled. The opportunity was so good that the new acquirer could not resign himself to sell the building. He took up residence therein, after his fashion. On his orders, the ground floor rooms, empty and sonorous, were locked. He had no use for them, only receiving his clientele—and none of his morning visitors, even if he had been speaking for an hour, could boat of ever receiving the succor of a glass of water. A manservant of sorts had the responsibility of tidying the garden, where, instead of flowers, meager cabbages and lettuces grew. The owner ate and slept in a sordid room under the eaves. Only the office was heated in winter, and furnished with a large table in carved oak, gothic friezes and assorted cupboards, which doubtless hid strongboxes. A stained-glass window of Medieval aspect diffused a sepulchral light. Instinctively, people talked in low voices in that lair, which my father deemed luxurious.

I arrived at 10 a.m. On the benches, awaiting their turn for strangulation, I found well-dressed young men who were hastily scanning pieces of paper covered with figures; inventors in patched-up rags; old ladies with handbags stuffed with summonses; one gentleman with the appearance of a rich businessman, but quivering with nervous tics; and three mendicants sent away by the faithful servant: "Monsieur greatly regrets that he has no time, and will never have time, for you. There is no point in coming back."

The clients went out by the door to the garden, which prevented those who had not yet been received from seeing the triumphant or furious expressions of the others. My turn finally arrived. I was admitted to the honor of a Gothic armchair that swallowed me. My godfather did not get up. He waved at me vaguely. For these audiences, he dressed in a solemn manner: beige woolen trousers, a sort of nocturnal smoking-waistcoat, and a cravat with a yellowish pin. He had to clip the prickles that served as his hair and beard himself. Although scantily nourished he was almost obese, and that water-drinker had the crimson face of a drunkard. As he suffered from a paralysis of the eyelids, he nimbly lifted up one eyelid with his forefinger when he judged it appropriate to look at his interlocutor—which is to say, as soon as he came in. After that, he offered nothing but a closed face.

"To what do I owe the honor?" he asked me.

I told him my little story.

"Oh!" he exclaimed. "Oh!" And he added: "A relative," as if he were crying; "A murderer!" He went on: "Raymond Portereau left France following an act of folly. You're undoubtedly unaware…an insignificant blunder: a few francs that he was supposed to be collecting on someone else's behalf, with which he ran off. He was only 15. Let's see—has he been successful?"

"Yes."

"So you haven't come to ask me for money?"

"No."

"Bravo. You've come to introduce yourself to me, to remind me of our family ties. I've very touched. Delighted to have seen you. Well done!"

"Monsieur," I said, "I will be grateful if you would not consider me as an intruder or a beggar. Your time is precious, as is mine. I'm settling in France. I have the intention to set up in business here on a large scale. My personal funds are inadequate; I therefore propose that you participate, to the extent that you judge appropriate."

"Will it be profitable?"

"You shall judge."

"You must have met, in the course of your travels, quite a few rich young men whose treasuries had become confused. In such cases, I charge ten per cent as an intermediary. I specialize in uncomplicating such dossiers."

I stopped him. "Those are the methods of 1830."

"They are good ones."

"This is another matter."

Félix-Amédée raised his eyelid once again, and kept it raised for five or six seconds in my honor, while he said: "Raymond had borrowed 700 francs from my father…"

"I can return them to you immediately." I paused, and added: "Do you have the receipt?"

This observation immediately put me in my godfather's good graces. "I wouldn't have mentioned it if I didn't have the receipt," he said. "I'll have to look for it in a pile of irrecoverable credits. We're in no hurry. You'll be coming back. I live alone, like an old wolf. Visits always give me pleasure, when they're not formalities of politeness, for appearances' sake. Speak— I'm listening. And don't be afraid of boring me."

My godfather followed the principle that anyone might bring something, and that even the vaguest person has at least one idea susceptible of yielding a profit, if applied by someone else. I must, in fairness, concede that he knew how to listen. Almost deprived of sight, he supplemented his visual sense with a highly developed auditory sense. To that end, nature had endowed him with enormous ears. So I spoke. I can only give a summary here of the speech in which I explained the progress realized by science and industry since 1896.

I began with the cinema: "It is destined," I said, "to a development of which you have no suspicion. Thousands of halls will open to the public and will make moving images a source of wealth comparable to wheat. I have, for example, the idea of animated drawings that will permit the realization of fairy tales, and I shall put specialist engineers on the track of colors that will give those drawings a singular life. The receipts of the cinema will be calculated in billions."

"Familiar!" Félix-Cyprien cut in.[12] "I never budge from here, but everything reaches me via my morning visitors. I estimate that this kind of magic lantern will ensure a few benefits to foreign merchants, and that's all. Foolishness!"

"But what about voyages? The documentation of the entire world?"

"They'll make the public yawn. Leave that invention to children. You're not expecting me to subsidize magic lantern shows?"

"Don't trust ready-made opinions, Monsieur, and formulas with which one is too easily content."

"Not a centime for the magic lantern!"

"Mechanical traction?"

"Velocipedes? Too many have already been made and the fashion has passed. The bicycle was queen in 1892. Since woman have disguised themselves in order to sit astride such instruments, they've fallen into ridicule…"

"Automobiles?"

"Can you sell them for 15 francs?"

"No."

"Then those people who are capable of investing more than 15 francs in a vehicle will always prefer horses. All this, my dear monsieur, if you want my ad-

---

[12] It is not obvious why the miser's name changes here.

vice, is buffoonery in which I wouldn't risk two *sous*. Give the taste of camembert to flour mixed with water and I shall say: 'I'm your man! Let's get started!'"

"The airplane?"

"The what?"

"The apparatus thanks to which men will fly."

"Can you show me one?"

"No."

"Right! My dear monsieur, I'm no smarter than anyone else. I think more carefully, that's all. And I think more carefully because I never let anything distract me. I've adapted, in my own fashion, the Latin adage *Homo sum!*[13] I'm a man, you understand. Not a woman! I leave crazes and dreams to women. In brief, I have my feet on the ground. We're relatives; I'll speak frankly to you: I expected better from you than obscure projects founded on an improbable future with which I'm overwhelmed every morning. One man has a roll of wax that reproduces sounds, and he expects mountains and marvels. A plaything. Send it back to the manufacturers in Nuremburg! Another makes use of photography for a kaleidoscope that shows a train entering a station. Plaything! Knick-knack! One can no more replace horses by machines than actors by their portraits. If we weren't cousins, I'd already have withdrawn my reverence. Without being indiscreet, have you a large fortune?"

"Not very large."

"Ah!"

---

[13] As the miser observes, *Homo sum* means "I am a man," but Duvernois undoubtedly expects his readers to know, and appreciate the irony of the fact, that the adage (from Terence) goes on: *humanum nihil a me alienum puto* [(therefore) nothing human is alien to me].

"An income of about 100,000 livres."

"Damn it, cousin!"

"It's nothing!"

"It's considerable. And how have you earned all that?"

"By looking for…"

"Ideas?"

"Ideas."

"Which you have applied?"

"In modest ways."

"And you want to expand?"

"Yes."

"Believe me, it's better to glean on a cultivated field. At your age, you can see the big picture? A snare of nature! In growing old, one becomes long-sighted, it seems, when it's much better to become short-sighted. Vast projects? The Future? Rubbish, my dear Monsieur, for you and for me. Have you anything else in your bag?"

"Yes, but they're trifles."

"If they're precise…"

"At hazard: what would you say to a portable pen with a reservoir that contains enough ink for a day's writing? The pen in gold…"

"Let it be iron and I'll consider the project. It's more my cup of tea."

"A patent for wrapping toothpicks and sugar-cubes in paper—which constitutes an undeniable progress from the viewpoint of hygiene."

"Not bad."

"Manufacturing a white, pink or red varnish for women that they can paint on their nails in order to avoid polishing?"

"They're crazy enough to adopt your varnish. Worth looking at!"

"An electrical apparatus that will curl their hair for twelve months?"

"Right!"

"A chemical substance designed to take the nicotine out of tobacco and render it harmless?"

"Do you have the formula for the substance?"

"No, but once the principle is found, any chemist can take on the job."

"Possible. Anymore?"

"It's my turn to speak frankly to you. I haven't said everything. I have many other discoveries in mind."

"A brain bubbling over, I'm sure…"

"But I'll only give them to you one at a time, and after success."

"I'll give it all some thought. Come back next week. I'll have the receipt; bring the 700 francs. I'll also consult specialists, and will tell you to what extent you can count on my collaboration. There's no point in approaching anyone else; even if they see you, they won't listen. They'll have gone to bed too late the previous evening. Me, off to bye-byes at 7 p.m.! Get up at 5 a.m., of course. Those fine gentlemen have another nap at midday. They gorge themselves with food in expensive restaurants and drink wine that obscure their understanding. They come back to snooze in their offices, which they leave at 5 p.m. From 5 till 7 p.m., they wear themselves out with society ladies who give them bills to pay. They go back to their offices, exhausted, to sign documents. After that, black suit, the theater, loose women or baccarat. They never have disposable assets. What makes me strong is that I have disposable assets and have always considered love as a mere bagatelle, and that work, for me, takes the place of everything, even family—without wishing to offend you."

He makes as if to get up to accompany me to the door. I dissuade him.

"Ah," he groans. "The head is still good but the legs! I don't expect I'll last much longer."

"You'll live to a ripe old age," I affirm.

"How do you know? You're not a doctor."

"I have a little medical knowledge."

"You can give me a consultation. Mine's excellent, and I don't pay him dear, but he'd a pessimist and a wastrel. He comes here in a fancy carriage—can you imagine? And he's so lazy that he doesn't even write a prescription. For my ten francs, I don't get a bit of paper…"

Inspired by affability, he emerges from his armchair—and I find him just as I saw him for the last time, congested and bent, a centenarian since 60, walking with little muffled steps, economizing his breath, hanging on to the furniture with one hand and lifting up his inert eyelid with the other.

"You haven't made the tour of the family?" he asks. "There's no longer much of it. The Camille Portereaus…be wary…"

"You have something against them?"

"Camille's a stupid and coarse individual. He and his wife live only for their son, my godson, a simpleton. They chose me as godfather not out of affection, but interest. In that respect I'm not a child, and I'd have liked nothing better than to take an interest in him. I don't make a habit of giving Christmas presents, but every year, on January 1, I used to send him something. Even his manner of taking it and stuffing it in his pocket, like a rag, revolted me! There's also a daughter, of whom I would have made a shop-girl, for she's fetching, and of whom they want to make a high society goose. They don't have a *sou*, but they wear gloves and dress in the latest fashion. Nothing would be easier than for me to find a place for the father and the son in one of my businesses—an immoral solution. You earn your daily bread by the sweat of your brow. Avoid them—they'll bring you nothing but annoyance. I would be obliged if you didn't mention me to them. I heard some very bad things about Forgeix and Levacourt, the employers and gods of that idiot Camille. When I passed them on to him, I thought he was going to slap me. They're defrauding the customs, into the bargain. It will all end in disaster, and I'll rub my hands in glee!"

I cannot prevent myself starting in surprise. He explained: "Camille Portereau I don't mind, Rose too; their daughter Lucie is nothing to me…but the other…"

"Maxime-Félix?"

"Yes, Félix—I would have liked to make him my pupil. He's a disappointment. He can't stand me, and I return the compliment. It's well worth avoiding the formality of January 1, when he thought it worthwhile as a child to show me his talents as a musician, sculptor and poet, and later, to deafen me with his eloquence. A dandy, I tell you, and a chatterbox. He must have entered into the borrowing phase. One encounters him with painted women. There's one to whom I won't take oranges when he's in prison."

"He won't go to prison."

"Yes he will!"

On the subject of his godson, Félix is inexhaustible. He sees him with his head shaved and livid, beneath the blade of the guillotine. "And I'm not mistaken!" he concludes. "Bear up! Until we meet again!" And, telling his servant to see me out, he commands: "Next!"

What the old man has told me about my godson re-conciles me with my double. I did not protest. Later, when I have made him a great deal of money, I shall treat my godfather as he deserves and I shall avenge us...

My feet carry me instinctively to the Rue des Arc-hives, where I am not expected until the day after tomor-row. As soon as I have acquired a little money, I shall look for an apartment in the neighborhood of the Porte-reau family. But how can I earn money right away? By opening a fortune-teller's booth? I have the feeling that my wonderful ideas will be received almost everywhere as Félix-Amédée has just received them...

At 60 years of age, rich back on Earth, I must think about earning my living here. I glimpsed infinite possi-bilities, but it will be much harder than I imagined. I am paying for my ignorance. For instance, I know some-thing about the principles of wireless telegraphy, but I would be incapable of constructing an apparatus or of giving a worthwhile explanation. In default of billions, I shall content myself with millions—nor for me, my ter-restrial self, but for my family and my double. Am I not going to reproach him, like my uncle the usurer, for hav-ing mistresses? Have I not, with regard to him—with regard to my youth—some obscure rancor?

IX.

In a little street in Neuilly, my attention has been caught by a humble shop on which I have read: *Guillard Dyers*.

Georgette has told me: "I was born in Neuilly."

I go on, on the pretext of asking for a price-list—and I see a child a few months old in a baby-carriage: a blonde baby with rosy cheeks and large clear blue eyes.

"He's superb!" I declare.

"She," the father corrects me, proudly. "That's our daughter. Give monsieur a nice wave, Georgette."

Georgette waves her little hand. I ask permission to kiss her. She receives my kiss—already!—indifferently, and grasps my umbrella, refusing to let go.

"Oh, she's strong!" observes the mother.

"Very strong," I agree. "She shows promise."

I tell them that I will send some clothes to be cleaned. My future mistress surrenders the umbrella sulkily. I make a rapid calculation. I would have thought that Georgette was younger! She wasn't really lying, though, when she said: "I've always had my carriage!"

She misses the umbrella...

Although I find myself in an exceptional situation, being the only human being to know the near future of the planet on which he moves...I'm bored. I know too many things. And I learn, sadly, that past a certain age, one is scarcely moved by anything except curiosity. Here, I have no curiosity.

Thus, I never read the newspapers. What would be the point? I pick up one at the hotel, however, which proves to be a racing paper. It publishes the fields for that afternoon—and I suddenly remember having been at Longchamp that day. Gomieux, claiming that he had "inside information" had marked six horses for me to bet on in blue pencil, which would pay off at good odds, and none of which was placed. With an effort, I recall the names of the winners: Redingote, Parmentier, Zanaïdella, Choc en retour, Manosse and Bébelle.

I shall go to Longchamp this afternoon.

The elegance of the paddock, as the mundane chroniclers put it: puffed sleeves, dresses with trains, vast hats, frills and boas; the gentlemen in stove-pipe hats, flowers I their buttonholes. Here comes an actress, then at the height of her glory, and a much sought-after minister, a celebrated crook who will end his days in prison and who passes by, superb and disdainful, with his court of parasites. Practical jokers of the era, those of whom people say, "What fine trick is he going to play today?" and who wear their hilarious attitude like a uniform: an alcoholic gaiety one step short of unconsciousness. One of them murmurs to a comrade, "Papa's dead, you know," momentarily adopts a sorrowful expression, as if he were putting himself on guard, and immediately expands in an even larger smile.

I seem to be watching insects dancing, drunk on sunlight, just as they are about to run into the hand that crushes them. And in spite of the gusts of iris that the women emit as they pass by, Longchamp, beneath a pure and bright sky, has an odor of the cemetery…

"I find you here!"

It's Fanny. In order to join me, she leaves a group of monocled clubmen. I ask her what she has done with Maxime.

"He must be on the lawn, spying on me," she tells me. "Don't look. I'll see him soon enough. Where I come from, to say that someone is pestering you, we say: 'He gets on my nerves.'[14] That it, more or less. What do you expect? Maxime gets on my nerves. He's always talking about uninteresting things—and he's too personal. And as a lover, you can have him! He has a whole apprenticeship to serve, and I can't be bothered—it makes me feel old. Hang on, don't turn round. I can see him. He's white…"

In spite of her plea, I turn round and I wave to my double, who gives me a grateful bow. And I go to find him on the lawn. I offer him entry into the paddock. He thanks me, rather suspiciously. I take him by the arm. I observe that I'm a little taller than he is—he hasn't finished growing…

"May I address you informally?"

"Of course."

"You can do the same with me."

"You think so?"

"Yes. Do you intend to bet?"

"A little…"

"I'll give you some good information."

---

[14] What Fanny says in the original is "*Il me leune,*" *leune* being a dialect version of *lune* [Moon], whose derivative verb relates to the influence that satellite is supposed to have on people's moods, especially when full. The emphasis placed on the regional pronunciation is intended to highlight Fanny's southern origin.

"If you'll permit…" He starts again. "If you'll permit, I can mark your card. I have exceptional inside information from my friend Gomieux."

"Where does he get it?"

"From owners and jockeys."

"Mine are reliable, you know—absolutely reliable."

He reads the names, shrugs his shoulders, and says: "No chance!"

Was I so peremptory? Undoubtedly. It's very annoying. I insist: "I suggest an accumulator. Have you a *louis*? If you haven't, I'll lend you one…"

"No, no thanks…"

"I'll meet you here after the last race…"

I know full well that I'm on to a sure thing. All the same, I await the arrival of Redingote. She comes in, to general amazement. I've bet ten *louis*; I've won 18,000 francs.

The last race finishes with the victory of Bébelle. I find myself in possession of a capital of 147,000 francs…

It is my intention to conceal this win. I shouldn't have marked Maxime's card. It's necessary, at all costs, that I pass unnoticed. The custom, if not of burning sorcerers, at least of imprisoning them, has not been entirely abolished.

"Well," Fanny cries out to me, "have you been lucky?"

"I had first-rate information. Unfortunately, as usual, I changed my mind at the last minute."

Maxime is downcast. He now has scarcely enough in his pocket for a second-class railway-ticket home. "I was wrong," he confesses, "not to listen to you."

"Bah! Sheer luck…shall we leave together?"

As Fanny goes to say goodbye to the gentlemen who brought her, I slip four 1000-franc notes into my double's pocket. "What are you doing?" he exclaims.

"Correcting fate. Pay me back when you can."

His confidence restored by the small fortune bestowed upon him, Maxime has but one irritation: that that of having to tolerate the presence of a third person. I liberate him from it. On the pretext of a forgotten rendezvous at the Porte Dauphine, I make myself scarce.

There is evidently a latent hostility between my double and me. However, I have always lived in accord with myself, and that was a consolation to me at times when the presence of my fellows became tedious.

At 8 p.m., I consult the theater posters. They are presenting *Faust, Le Fils de l'Aretin, La Vivandière, Pour la couronne, Le Carnet du Diable* and *La Mendiante de Saint-Sulpice*. I decide in favor of the Renaissance and *Amants*. I savor it in its freshness—which will endure—the winged grace of Maurice Donney's tender and poetic fantasy, with the great Lucien Guitry and the adorable Jeanne Granier.[15] A lesson in indulgence and irony...

---

[15] Duvernois presumably checked the theater listings in his old newspaper; the 1859 opera *Faust* and the 1844 ballet *La Vivandière* were standard items of the repertoire; all the other titles mentioned premièred in 1895. *Le Fils de l'Aretin* is by Hebnri de Bornier, *Pour la couronne* by François Coppée, the comic opera *Le Carnet du Diable* by Ernest Blum and Paul Ferrier and *La Mendiante de Saint-Sulpice* by Xavier de Montepin, hastily adapted from his successful feuilleton serial. It is not at all surprising that Duvernois sent his protagonist to the Théâtre de la Renaissance to watch *Amants*, by his good friend Maurice Donnay, which was a key work in pioneering the kind of "sophistication" in regard to sexual relationships that

I shall not struggle against my destiny, which is that of a parasite. I had hoped to exploit to my benefit a blind society forty years in arrears, make an immense fortune thanks to the inventions of others with which I am supplied in bulk, and dedicate that fortune to the general wellbeing. Now, I must content myself with gains made at Longchamp races, and if I try to play the prophet, it might cook my goose…

I would give many of the months that I still have to live to know what has happened on Earth since my departure. I suppose that if the apparatus had projected me further, I would have arrived on a world more than a hundred years older…which would probably not be better or more interesting. There must be a whole set of twin planets of that sort, and, higher still and further away, the unknown that is closed to us by the divine will, by reason of unworthiness. I find myself, in sum, in a sort of backward suburb.

I could happily spend the night walking under the stars, but there are no stars. A fine and persistent rain is falling, which chills my bones. At a given point, a door opens, sending me a gust of laughter and music.

---

was to become Duvernois' hallmark as a popular writer central to the fashions of his era. The play is perhaps best-known today because of the fine poster produced for its publicity by Alphonse Mucha, but that was done for its American tour (when it was put on by Sarah Bernhardt's company) so Maxime will have seen something more prosaic. Duvernois was presumably well acquainted with the Renaissance's director, Lucien Guitry, whose son Sacha—a notable actor himself, especially in films—was one of the co-founders of *Oeuvres Libres*.

This is the place where the day's winners meet—and the losers too, desirous of numbing themselves. The orchestra is playing a slow waltz, dedicated to the ladies who are becoming languid, while their companions, are getting drunk and picking quarrels. Two or three leaders are directing the saraband. While the violins draw out their syrupy melody, revelers break glasses and plates, the pieces of which the resigned waiters pick up and ask respectfully: "On whose bill should they be put, please?" Foreigners who would be very reserved in their own countries play the role here of mercenary soldiers who break everything on the eve of a victory. They hesitate between kisses and murder.

Monsieur Forgeix, in a black suit and an over-stretched shirt, with his cravat askew, is sharing a table of honor with Monsieur Levacourt and two small women reminiscent of whipped and peevish bitches. He calls me over. Am I alone? Yes. Well then, the more the merrier! And when he has introduced me and sat me down, he pushed us along to make room for a newcomer, in whom I recognize a statesman currently exiled to the shadows, who is planning his revenge. We fraternize.

The politician, who has come from an electoral banquet, explains that he is not familiar with pleasure spots, but that his wife is in the provinces, that he needs to know everything, and that since his—temporary!—retreat he has become a naturalized Parisian. Monsieur Forgeix whispers his filth in the ear of his companion, who roars with laughter on cue and repeats: "You could say that you're an old devil!" without further explanation. Monsieur Levacourt, more correct, does the honors of this place where he reigns as master to the other small woman, who is visibly searching for something to steal: the silvered metal pepper-pot, the golden cigarette-case that Monsieur Levacourt picks up and prudently puts in his pocket, our watch-chains, the drinking-straws, the ash-trays, or anything at all…

The ex-statesman talks to me about his projects. As he is bound to return to power, I try to furnish him with a few tips, and lift a corner of the veil for him—not so much that he will cry "implausible!" but enough for him to remember my clairvoyance at a later date. He shakes his head and gets up. Have I enthused him? No. He murmurs "Excuse me" and, dressed like a notary, with his spectacles balanced on his nose and his large electoral paws beating the air, performs an agile solo dance. The public cheers. He searches on all fours for his spectacles, which have fallen off during this crisis of saltation, and, as one of his lenses is cracks, makes a semblance of bursting into tears. Forgeix's young companion, desirous of proving her talents, bring out a handkerchief, with which she sponges the improvised dancer's forehead. "You don't find him funny? Me, I think he's very funny."

He takes his place again next to me, returns his conquest to Forgeix and says to me: "These young folk no longer know how to have fun! They bellow, that's all. Monsieur, I've listened to you. I want to reply…"

He speaks to me, a little, and to the neighboring tables, a great deal—and I gather that he was preparing this speech while feigning to listen to mine. I shall never make a dent in this block of vanity. By the time tomorrow proves me right, he will have forgotten everything I've said. But I approve—I approve entirely.

I have rented a furnished apartment in my parents' neighborhood. I have recovered an appetite for reading that I thought I had lost. I buy books from Messieurs

Husseaume. I shut myself up at home, a pretentious apartment in which the piano, the mantelpiece and even the tables are skirted with beige velvet. The padded interior of a dusty casket!

I am a fingernail sketch of Mirabeau's remark: "At the age of three, I preached; at six, I was a prodigy; at 12 an object of hope; at 20, a firebrand. At 40, I'm no more than an old man…"

I have run into my sister Lucie. We have walked a little way together. I ask her to confide in me; I assure her of my friendship. She manifests a reserved gratitude.

At the time, I scarcely knew her. I had my domain, she had hers. Later, she displayed a sordid cupidity, but there might have been something else…

I know nothing of the simple and complicated soul of a young woman tightly bound by bourgeois ties, who longs to escape from ennui as from a prison.

At first, she doesn't confess her love for Alexandre Pioulette, but she talks to me about him at length, which is tantamount to a confession. The young man is an impressionist painter by personal taste, but for the sake of establishing his situation, he places himself under the guidance of official daubers. His masters are chosen from among those painters of standardized portraits that depict senior magistrates in red robes and businessmen's wives in blue dresses. They approve of him, when he does not show them his own productions, which make them sigh: "What a pity! Such an intelligent boy!" Alexandre Pioulette is over 30. I imagine that on Earth, in 1936, he would seem behind the times; in 1896, he passes for a revolutionary. Lucie does not get mixed up in art, but all her sentimental possibilities are limited to Alexandre Pioulette. She believes that romance will remain unique in her life, and wants to read a few more lines of it…

"Haven't you ever thought of marrying him?" I insinuate. "Tell me—I'm capable of arranging many things."

"Thank you, cousin, but even money can't arrange everything…"

"However…"

"Alexandre has the best intentions in the world. For me, he would immediately undertake to represent beautiful dowagers as goddesses, or reel off sunsets by the score…but he would have a mediocre vocation. He wouldn't succeed in commerce, and I wouldn't want him to. For the moment, it's understood that he prefers me to his art, but preferences of that sort aren't eternal. And even if I had a small dowry, it would be necessary to resign myself to becoming an artist's wife, less well-dressed than his models, who must, in order to balance her budget, choose between the purchase of tubes of paint and that of a nice hat or a pair of shoes. He's crazy…he talks about trying something else, or going abroad. He begs me to wait for five or six years…. To tell you the truth, in the depths of my heart, I've given up on him." She concludes: "Life is serious!"

I try to disabuse her. No, not so serious, fundamentally. I sense that the terrible woman born in her, that calculating miser, only triumphed conclusively after sentimental disappointment. She is reproaching her hero for not having given her precise orders. He pleases her, but he has not subjugated her. She would make the sacrifice of her youth for her husband's glory if he affirmed that glory to be infallible—but he isn't sure, and he even feels, on occasion, an abortive discouragement. "Perhaps he has talent when he's in front of a canvas; elsewhere, he's a weakling." And at the end of the day, when one is named Pioulette, one must cover that name in glaring luster, or else seem ridiculous.

"I'll encourage him to leave—but at his own risk and peril. I shan't make him any promise, swear any oath. Since it's necessary for me to fight alone, I shall fight for myself."

"What does your brother think?"

Lucie looks at me. She thinks my illusions with regard to Maxime very naïve. "My brother? Thanks to him," she explains, "I know men. I only have to watch him live to measure their egotism. My brother—but Maxime has been very nearly what Alexandre is, but younger, for he's precocious. And what has he become? If someone in the house is ill, he declares, on principle, that they will get better. Things will always get better.

"He knows what Alexandre's intentions are. He knows that fundamentally—yes, fundamentally—I have a broken heart, and he avoids any conversation on that subject. He doesn't like anything that saddens him, and when he realizes that I want to talk to him about anything except the weather, he grabs the first pretext to get away. It's necessary that everything should sort itself out without him, without his intervention, without anyone asking him to do anything, make any effort or reflect for five minutes.

"If I hadn't lived with my brother, if I hadn't observed him, I'd have been Alexandre's wife a long time ago—but I think of my dear brother's flashes of genius. Perhaps he was a composer as the other is a painter. Was it life that stopped Maxime? I don't think so. He was stopped by his own limitations. Look—I've known him to be very good; he has had his crisis of generosity as he had his crisis of musical genius. It passed. He still thinks he's good, but that's an error on his part, an illusion with which he flatters himself because it suits him. He's not wicked, that's all.

"If he heard me, he'd fall over backwards, or slap me to show me that I'm mistaken and that he's tender and devoted. Mama is exquisite. She has carried over to him all the illusions that she has lost with respect to my father—and he fortifies them. For both of them, one cannot be a man like other men when one has been a child prodigy. Thus, at school, some of my comrades seem phoenixes in the infant classes; they were heaped with compliments and prizes—and having acquire a solid reputation, they became idiots. All that makes me cry, sometimes, you know—but even tears don't prevent me from seeing clearly."

I hated Lucie. I absolve her. No one ever reached out to that gloomy little soul, closed and realistic by obligation. There was no one to pay attention to her but that poor painter—a quibbler, in effect. And she is lucid. She has just, without a doubt, landed me with some hard home truths, albeit retrospectively. She asks me for secrecy, which I promise. And we talk about something else. I have her friendship, insofar as she is capable of feeling friendship.

I try to buy her a brooch that I point out to her in a jeweler's shop-window. She refuses. "Later, when I have nice dresses." She doesn't want anything except a bouquet of violets. Does she suspect the purity of my intentions?

X.

I have made a large purchase at Forgeix and Leva-court's. I didn't haggle, but I specified that a commission must be given to Monsieur Camille Portereau. Thus, indirectly, I shall come to the aid of my parents. My father will only be grateful to his employers, who will never again be able to reproach him for never having helped them sell a centimeter of cloth.

I arrive early for dinner, and I find my mother admiring a spray of roses that I have had sent to her.

"I don't have the courage to scold you," she says. "I love flowers so much! What a pity they're a luxury! You're spoiling us too much, my dear André. Lucie told me that you wanted to buy her some jewelry…" She explains: "You know that she's almost engaged to a young painter, Alexandre Pioulette. It's only provisional; I don't think it's reasonable, but what seems to me more unreasonable still is a loveless marriage—in which there is, for example, a disparity in age…"

That point is intended for me. My solicitude for the family is being attributed to the excessively lively interest that Lucie inspires in me! I need to dispel that error.

"Marry them off quickly," I say. "He has talent, it seems, and poverty is only frightful when one has does not have for its support the radiance of youth, work to do and a family to found. Marry them. I'll do my best to help them."

My mother breathes easy. That suspicion is set aside. I'm merely a sentimental old boy, perhaps weary of restaurant food. She thanks me for what I've just said. The ice has melted. I find myself bathed in tenderness, as when I was very small and took refuge by her side, prey to some chagrin that she would dissipate with a kiss. Beware—I'm about to let the truth slip out, losing my mastery of what I am saying; my unconscious self will reveal the incredible…

A subterfuge saves me. "I had a dream last night that I must relate to you."

"Please do," says my mother, and blinks in a familiar fashion, as she used to do when I talked childish nonsense to her. "But how emotional you are, about a nightmare?"

"Not a nightmare: one of those absurd but surprising dreams that leave the impression on awakening, even upon the most hardened materialist, that there is something else…"

"I hope you're not a materialist?"

"Yes and no…"

"How terrible! How can we live, if life is all there is!" My mother has let that exclamation slip out, and immediately regrets it.

"You're not happy, then, Rose?"

"I've never asked myself that question. I have the best of husbands, delightful children…quickly, your dream…"

And I can tell the truth, in that form. "I was on another planet…"

"More beautiful than this one, probably."

"No!"

"Then it's hardly worth the trouble of dreaming!"

"The same as this one, but forty years further advanced…"

"War was abolished? A means had been found of never growing old? Not dying, perhaps? Money ceased to be tyrannical and everyone in the world could eat and stay warm?"

"Is that how you see the future? Alas, Rose, progress does not move so quickly. It proceeds by slow, blind steps. There was still the threat of war. Growing old and dying were not things of the past. Only a few trivia, in means of distraction and locomotion, gave the people pride in belonging to their epoch. What's more, the old had no lack of regret for the mildness of yours...of ours..."

"That wouldn't be difficult!"

"Thus, I found myself, as you see me at this moment, alone and virtually useless, prudently administering a fortune that I hadn't earned, without which I would have found myself in greater difficulty than the meanest of vagabonds—in essence, caught between a desire for action that no longer corresponded with my strength, and the desire to put an end to that monotonous farce...."

"Then an inventor offers me the means to undertake, at my own risk and peril, an extraordinary exploration, to go and see what is happening in the vicinity of Proxima Centauri, the nearest star. As a child I had a mania for contemplating the firmament..."

"Like Maxime! We thought for a long time that he would become an astronomer..."

"The apparatus having been constructed, I escape...it takes a long time, a very long time...I travel through a kind of fiery night. And suddenly: daylight. I'm on another planet, but it's exactly like the one I've left, forty years earlier!"

"There's always a moment when a dream becomes stupid. It's the one when the human imagination comes into play and breaks the enchantment with an incongruous detail. I'm quite content never to dream. The most poetic dream is always impeded by stupidities."

"So I've arrived in a world that I remember. I see again the dear individuals that I have lost. I'm an old man, and I confront my young mother, who does not recognize me…"

"Ah! At that moment you should have woken up. A mother always recognizes her child…"

"I find myself facing myself, my t20-year-old self, who seems to me to be full of conceit and stupidity. I know, and I find myself among people who do not know. I bring progress; no one listens to me. They make fun of me…"

"That's where the nightmare begins…"

"Yes, Rose, you're right: the worst of nightmares. A stranger for whom it is impossible to give any proof of what has happened to him, under pain of being taken for a madman. He cannot be loved, either amorously, in friendship or simple affection. He simply comes to re-gret not being dead. He thought he could solve the puz-zle; he does indeed know what others do not know, but the mystery remains intact. He has passed from one grain of sand to another. He has made the expedition of an ant, proud to have gone a few meters further than the habitual journeys of other ants…"

"And then? Someone came to bring you your break-fast! But you're still under the influence of this night-mare. Pinch yourself. I mean it—pinch yourself hard."

I obey.

"Finished!" concludes my mother, laughing. "We're in 1896, and as I don't have a numerous staff, I shall have to go see what's happening in the kitchen, under pain of offering you a bad dinner—which would be too much, after a bad night. Maxime won't be long. I'll send you Lucie. She likes you a lot."

And you, Rose—do you like me a little?"

"That goes without saying."

She is fearful of my effusiveness. At the end of a stuff arm she gives me her hand to kiss, squeezes mine rapidly and disappears.

I can never go any further in my confidences. Never.

Alexandre Pioulette has brought Lucie a picture that he has just painted: a spring landscape, a suburban backwater excused by a bright sky and enchanted by fishermen and cherry-trees in flower. He's a very mild, very slender young man with the hands of a workman and the eyes of an artist. One senses that he is fearful of all judgments.

"Isn't it pretty, cousin?" Lucie asks, without conviction.

"Marvelous!"

"Oh!" murmurs Picoulette, blushing. "Marvelous!"

"I want to give you proof of my sincerity; I shall come to see you and buy a painting from you, which will bring a little sunlight into my new apartment."

"That's too kind," stammers Pioulette. "If you like this kind of painting, I can point you in the direction of a comrade who had much more talent than me, and whom no one encourages."

"Are buyers forming a queue at your studio, then?" Lucie asks, ironically, looking at me as if to say: "You see what he's like!"

But Forgeix has just come in. The sight of the painting makes him laugh. "A joke!" he cries. "The young man is a clown. You have to laugh at it in order not to be irritated. My friend, do you think that the good God created fruit trees for you to expose them to derision? If you want to make a caricature, take my face, for example, but leave the trees in peace, Monsieur, leave them in peace…"

Maxime intervenes. I await his verdict. He is sharply critical of a mauve shadow. He has never seen a mauve shadow. I interject: "Perhaps that's because you haven't looked properly?"

"Oh! I beg your pardon. I have the pretension…"

"And perhaps also because you don't know anything."

General stupor. My mother, who has just come in, starts painfully. I have just committed a crime of lèse-Maxime.

"And me too—I don't know anything, then?" exclaims Forgeix.

"No, my dear Monsieur."

Everyone is against me, including the painter, who promises to do better, to apply himself, to please everyone with appropriate paintings. He does not want to be at odds with the family oracle, Maxime. My father tries to bring everyone into accord by excusing Pioulette as a beginner. According to him, he will certainly make the career in art of those politicians who begins as anarchists and finish up ministering sugar-water.

I take Pioulette to one side. "If you listen to them," I say, "you're doomed!"

"The terrible thing," he tells me, "is that my masters and comrades share their opinion."

"Get it into your head that you have no masters and that your comrades are either cretins or envious. Being ill-natured is the only way to have a nature."

He smiles without replying. He has more confidence in these ignoramuses than in himself—or in me, of course. And he goes to hide his painting in the hallway.

The feast begins. The kitchen-maid has been disguised as a lady's-maid, she has been informed that she will be empty-handed if she says anything incongruous. "Dinner is served, Madame!"

My mother summons my father, who has taken Monsieur Forgeix into a corner and is talking to him fervently about the business. "Camille," she says, "it's ready!"

The maid, thinking that she has made a mistake, tries again: "Camille, it's ready!"

Everyone laughs and goes into the dining-room. The silver candlesticks, a legacy from a well-of great-grandmother, which are brought out on important occasions, are lit. That is a solemnity. I would have been so happy to be there without the presence of Monsieur Forgeix and Pioulette.

I am seated beside my mother. She divides herself equitably between Monsieur Forgeix and me, while my father addresses himself solely to the Boss, who treats him with abundant condescension. From time to time, he sends me little signals of complicity: we are the rich men among these little people. Maxime only takes part in the conversation when he can slip in a veiled reference to Fanny: "They're making magnificent dresses at the moment, pearled in red." Lucie looks after Pioulette, who eats little, desirous of not appearing too hungry and encouraging the belief that he dines like this every evening.

I pity them all—even Forgeix. After dinner, we listen, he makes a speech standing up. He deigns to declare himself satisfied with the meal. "But I said soup and beef. What good is braised pike? Another time, boil it.

Isn't that so, Monsieur André? For everything else, we have the great restaurateurs."

At 11 p.m., the session ends. Maxime offers to see me home. Pioulette tears himself away from Lucie as if he were leaving her forever.

"Meaning no reproach," she says, rather cruelly, "that's three times that you've said goodbye to me!"

In the street, Maxime informs me that he has promised Fanny to take me to her place. "She even asked me for your address so that she could invite you. You'll find the telegram at home."

I plead fatigue, and an urgent meeting that requires me to get up very early in the morning. I submit to another eulogy to Fanny.

"What about the other one?" I ask.

"Choute? Oh, no! What do you expect me to talk about with Choute?"

"And with Fanny?"

"She's has an extraordinary intelligence, such as I've rarely encountered in a woman."

Poor Maxime! Poor me! "Good luck to you, then."

"Why good luck?"

"Yes, yes—go find her. Hurry!"

"She'll be annoyed with me for not having brought you. She likes you so much that I'm a little ticked off, I can tell you…"

"An old man!"

"You aren't that old," he retorts, politely. Then he consults his watch and leaps into a cab—but a silhouette emerges from the shadows.

"You!" I exclaim. It's Choute. She's been following us. She apologizes—but she didn't dare disturb us.

"How did you know that he'd be here?"

She often goes past his house. She saw the windows lit up. Then she waited. "Tell me, Monsieur, where has he gone?"

"A lecture on Chemistry, I think, or Geography…"

"Don't worry—I don't want to delay you any longer…"

As it happens, I don't know what became of Choute when I abandoned her. To soothe my conscience, I imagined her married, with children, having become a stout bourgeois wife, very tranquil, with no regrets or remorse…but it sometimes also happens that a little cadaver is discovered in a tiny apartment, with a letter: "Let no one be blamed for my death. I've had enough." I cannot let Choute go like this. She is trembling too much. The weather is fine; I take her for a walk.

"I think," she remarks, "that you have his voice. Not surprising, since you're related…"

"Close your eyes, then, and imagine that it's him who is here."

I question her. She's certainly a little depressed at the moment: the braid-seller who gives her work is retiring, his fortune made, and his successor has his own favorites. "When I bring my black braid, he pulls it so hard that it always tears and tells me to learn to do it properly. I almost said to him: 'Try that with the others, and see if their braid doesn't break…'"

Little by little, she grows bolder. Beneath my arm, hers is no longer trembling. And beside her, listening to that little singsong voice from the depths of my past, I'm suddenly my double's age. I feel a sad sensuality. For her, it's no longer the aged cousin that is accompanying her, but Maxime himself, reverted to his original gentleness, when he set out to seduce her, when he said: "Forever, my dear, isn't it? Forever?"

"Come in for a moment. You trust me, I suppose?"

"Oh! Yes, Monsieur."

"We'll be able to chat more comfortably then, and I'll see you home."

She follows me—the only link that attaches her to Maxime. Perhaps she'll come back for me? She thinks my apartment splendid. The beige velvet of the curtains and the fringes on the mantelpiece and the piano seem to her to be the last word in luxury and taste. I light a kerosene lamp, which covers us with soot. I install Choute in an armchair. And as the lamp gets even smokier, I put it out. We're lit by the moon.

I install myself on a stool at her feet, and I tell her all the things that I ought to have told her before: not that I love her, of course—she would laugh at me—but that her presence enchants me.

"I'm scarcely educated…"

"So much the better!"

"I went to the state school…"

"I know. Brought up by an old aunt who beat you…"

"Yes…"

"And to whom you said: 'I don't have a vocation to be a child-martyr'…"

"He told you all that? So he thinks about me when I'm not there?"

"How do you expect him to forget you…Ville-d'Avray, Choute."

"I wasn't Choute yet, then. I was…"

"You were Amélie."

"What! Even that!"

"I'm well-informed!"

"I thought he'd forgotten it. He must have told you that he didn't think the name Amélie very pretty."

"It's delightful."

"He baptized me Choute."

"Which is frightful."

"Oh no, Monsieur—it depends on the way it's pronounced."[16]

"Amélie!"

She shivers. "It's curious, all the same, that you could have his voice. But what would he say if he saw us together, as we are right now?"

"He would be furious."

"I'm not so sure…"

I was, until my arrival on the planet Celia, a confirmed egotist. I should like to live a little longer, to live for myself and not for others. I confuse the old man worn out by so many quilted years and the adolescent who collects his first loving kiss from the lips of his first mistress—and I think that she is confused too, aided by the obscurity, moved by my voice, which is that of the other…

A troubled silence…

I shake myself.

A little more, and I would betray Maxime! Betray myself! I should protect this girl, without demanding anything in exchange but a little compassion, a little

---

[16] The French *chou*, the literal meaning of which is "cabbage," is often used as a term of endearment, but "Choute" is also somewhat suggestive of *chouette*, whose literal meaning is "owl" but which is used to signify "old hag," and the interjection *Chut!*, which is the equivalent of the English "Shh!" The nickname is, therefore, more than a trifle equivocal, and much would, indeed, depend on its exact pronunciation.

friendship, Besides, she'd only give in to me out of annoyance, out of spite…

"It's late," I say. "Come on, child—I'll take you home. You need your sleep…"

XI.

Fatality: it is written that I shall betray my double—if one can call that treason. Fanny has come to my apartment in search of my reply to the letter of invitation she sent me on the evening of the dinner at my parents' house.

"A basket of orchids isn't a reply. I suspect Maxime of having put you off, or at least of not having insisted, as he should have. My dear friend, how sad your home is! It needs a woman's touch…"

While she chatters, fundamentally rather awkward in her approach, and less cheerful than usual, I summon up my memories. What is destined to become of her? I seem to remember that, old and wealthy, she acquired a regrettable penchant for poor but impulsive adolescents, and was found one morning murdered in her fine majestic bed.

She lies down coquettishly on my settee and I suddenly see her, her throat slashed by the thrust of a knife, the blackness of the blood bringing out the false redness of her hair, and the atrocious smile on her blue lips exposing her teeth…

"What are you thinking about, André?"

"Give me your hand."

"Are you going to tell my fortune?"

"Yes?"

"Do you know how?"

"Well enough."

"I've always been told that I would meet a violent death."

"Indeed. That sign, however, is only a warning…"

"I need to be wary?"

"Yes."

"Tell me, my dear friend, don't you think it just that one should die for love, having lived for it? I won't make old bones—so much the better! Short and sweet, that's my motto. I've been half-strangled once already—not Maxime, poor Maxime always stops at threats! I had a paper-knife within arm's reach; I could have used it to defend myself; I didn't make a move. Then he relaxed his grip, and started to cry, complaining that I had treated him as a dish-rag!"

Gradually, she takes me into her confidence. She tells me everything that she has hidden from Maxime. More sincere with me than with him, she wants to bare herself, body and soul. I embody, perhaps by virtue of my gentleness and the interest I show in her, everything that attracted her to the other at the beginning of their liaison.

"Does it annoy you," she asks me, "that I'm putting myself at ease? Oh, you don't make me feel uneasy. It's as if I'd always known you. You're sure that we've never met before?"

"Certain. I would have remembered."

"Oh. I'm so ordinary, deep down, you know…"

Is that a blast of my youth rising to my head and intoxicating me? Is it an obscure desire to live for myself again? More likely the latter. While she calmly gets undressed, I sit down at the piano.

"That tune…" She murmurs.

One of Maxime's tunes: the little sonata that I composed as a child—"He's Mozart!"—and arranged subsequently. I played it on Earth when I was alone and wanted to evoke cherished phantoms.

"Don't you know anything else?"

I replace the work of Maxime-Félix Portereau, advantageously, by a Chopin *étude*. Then I stop. Fanny's perfume, that of an inebriating bouquet when one unwraps the paper the covers it...to breathe it once more...to strip an elegant woman of 1896, with her petticoats and corset, of so many complicated accessories...

She laughs nervously when I cover shoulder—which retains the innocent roundness of a child's—with kisses.

"I feel so stupid next to you," she confides. "So I'm not as stupid as all that, am I?"

Indeed—and it's me who becomes so. Nothing else exists any longer. I'm no longer thinking about my double, who was not wrong to be suspicious of me. That imbecile—who still has so many years to live—is a matter of indifference to me. The old passion grips me again...

"I'll wager that you have three little beauty spots in a triangle beneath your left breast."

"You've won! We really have already met, you see—I was sure of it. But when? Where?"

"And a scar on your hip..."

"I tell people that I fell on a stone when I was a child...I fell on a knife, but much later, in Mont-de-Marsan,[17] actually...a poor fellow that I didn't want. He said: 'Well, you won't be anyone else's!' He stabbed me, and afterwards, I had to hold him back—he wanted to throw himself into a well. 'What is it you would have killed, after all?' I said to him. 'A whore. That's not worth killing yourself for!'"

---

[17] Mont-de-Marsan is the capital of the Landes department in Aquitaine, in south-west France; the reference confirms Fanny's provincial origin.

What is a drama for the common run of mortals seems pure farce to Fanny. She might well have burst out laughing in the face of the murderer who nailed her to her bed of state forever and encouraged him: "Go on! What are you killing, after all?' Besides, by virtue of the physical details that I've already given her, she's convinced that I've already had her. "Have you ever passed yourself off as someone named Simon?"

At about 6 p.m., she goes to the window and lifts up the curtain.

"He's there!" she cries. "Maxime has followed me. He's there. He's pacing up and down outside the door."

The house has two exits. Fanny can leave by the service stairs.

"But what about him?" she says. "He'll ask you for an explanation…"

"Don't worry about it."

"He wants to fight duels with everyone."

"He won't fight me."

"Do you want me to go and see him and beg him to leave us alone?"

"No, I'll take care of him."

"I'm sure he doesn't scare you, but it's necessary not to push people too far."

She lets the curtain fall and finally leaves, but anxiously. "I always have to cause trouble…." And she is gone.

I tidy up the apartment. Then I go back to the window. Maxime is still there. Suddenly, he comes to a decision, plunges toward the front door, head down, and rings the doorbell imperiously. I open the door and assume my most natural tone.

"Why, it's you?"

"You aren't expecting me?"

"You aren't addressing me as *tu* any longer?"

"No. Where is she?"

"Who?"

"Fanny. You're not going to pretend that she isn't here. I saw her come in."

"Take a look. You don't seem to me to be your normal self."

He makes a rapid tour of the apartment and comes back empty-handed. "Of course," he explains. "You spotted me—the house must have two exists. The world is upside-down—it's the young man who is cuckolded! Have you the effrontery to deny it?"

"I shan't give you an answer."

"You're a dirty old man, and I don't know what's stopping me from slapping you across the face."

"The notion of ridicule, perhaps?"

"In any case, I beg you to consider yourself slapped."

"If that's all that will satisfy you, fine: I've been slapped."

"I'll expect your seconds."

"Don't."

"So you're a filthy coward?"

"I'm not a filthy coward, but I find dueling grotesque."

"Do you prefer corporal punishment?"

"Quite frankly, no."

"I beg you not to take that tone with me."

"Then take another yourself."

"If it's a matter of the 4000 francs that you lent me…"

"You're going to give them back?"

"I'll reimburse you."

"No hurry. Take of your hat and listen. Fanny came to talk to me about you. She hopes that I would be able to convince you…"

"Of what?"

"That a gallant man who is not loved must understand, resign himself to it, and not regret what has been given to him by virtue of the persistence with which he demanded more. That woman is not for you, Maxime. It happens that there is, in the shadows, another who is waiting for you, and whom you have driven to despair. You no longer want her—so be it. Imagine that she were pursuing you, persecuting you—and you will understand your own error…"

"I'm not a little girl…"

"You're a poor little beginner."

"Ah! Obviously, if I had your experience and your money…"

"Do you want it?"

"Your money? No."

"I've seen Fanny. Nothing will change her—and since you want to know everything, I've seen Choute too. I comforted her…"

"What right have you to interfere? You come here, having fallen out of the sky…" He never said a truer word. He continues: "And under the pretext of some vague relationship…no one has ever taken it into their heads to teach me a lesson."

"That's because no one is interested in you, except for your father and mother, who know nothing about your life."

"I can boast of having friends."

"It is a boast. One has no friends when one expects everything from them without offering anything in return. One has no true love when one takes a mistress as

135

if you were hiring a tradesman to bring you on an appointed day the happiness that you desire, neither more nor less. It's either necessary to settle for having only that which one purchases..."

"Which is your situation."

"Which is my situation...or to merit the rest, the admirable remainder: amity, passion..."

"I thank you for that lecture."

"You're very welcome."

"I shall verify what you have just told me."

"On the subject of friends?"

"On the subject of Fanny. And if you have lied, I shall never see you again, I warn you."

"I've invited your parents to dinner on Thursday."

"I'll find an excuse. For the 4000 francs, I suggest a monthly payment."

"Agreed: five francs a month; that way we shall remain in communication for a long time."

Maxime is nonplussed. I continue: "As for the duel, give up that idea. I have no intention of using you as a target or getting stabbed with a sword. How many times do I have to tell you that I consider you as another version of myself? That permits me to judge you objectively and talk to you frankly. Maxime, there are fine ideas and noble works..."

"As Juliette said to Jean-Jacques Rousseau: 'Let women alone and study mathematics...'"[18]

---

[18] This quotation, recorded in Rousseau's *Confessions*, is attributed to a Venetian lady of easy virtue named Ziulietta, who allegedly made the catty remark (in Italian) when the young Rousseau had a panic attack and was unable to perform as invited.

He has sat down. He is consumed by rancor, like a child who is no longer grief-stricken but still sighing.

"Your hand, Maxime?"

"Very well." Magnanimously, he shakes the hand that I offer him, limply. "Don't think I'm crying," he tells me, taking out his handkerchief and mopping his eyelids.

"As if you would!"

"I don't cry, but…"

I remember! "Your eyes are watering?"

"Yes, all the time. It's incomprehensible."

"Look at me. Yes, I'm not mistaken—those little spots on your cheeks. You have the measles."

"Never!"

"Go home, quickly, go to bed and have the doctor summoned."

"Measles! A childhood disease! People my age don't get it…"

"You're only a child. Keep well wrapped-up."

I did, indeed, have a late bout of measles.

"Oh!" cries Maxime, for whom Fanny is passing into the background, "I sense that I shall die…"

"You won't die. A week in bed, another week in your room, and you'll be dancing around as before."

No, no—I have a fever. I feel very ill…" And he begs: "Don't leave me…"

I have brought a Maxime green with terror back home to his mother. Green *and* red…

"Above all, Rose, don't torment yourself. It's nothing."

"Of course it's nothing," my mother says, "but I'm going to fetch the doctor. He lives in the building…"

Maxime is put to bed…

My room, where I spent delightful hours when I was a child: the cheerful flowered wallpaper; the little table at which, ten times in all, I worked to the point of exhaustion, feverishly and proudly; my books neatly arranged on the mahogany shelf; the portrait of my mother as a young woman, who still smiles in 1932 at her decrepit child…

Here comes doctor Hagiotte: frock coat, violet ribbon in the buttonhole and, to make up for his youth, a professorial beard and spectacles.

"Here's our invalid!" exclaims my mother, in a tone of fake cheerfulness. "He took ill a little while ago. Our cousin, who brought him home, affirms that he has the measles."

"Is Monsieur a colleague?" asks Dr. Hagiotte with stinging irony.

"I don't have that honor."

"Permit me, then, to make my own diagnosis."

He sits down unhurriedly. He asks questions, carries out a thorough examination. Evidently, he does not often find such a windfall. After mature reflection, he asks: "What did you eat for lunch?"

"Cutlets and fried potatoes."

"No fish?"

"No."

"And yesterday, for dinner?"

"Lobsters."

"We have it!" He searches for a scientific expression that will give value, and finds one. "Crustaceans are the root of all evil." He smiles agreeably. "My colleague improvised on seeing the young man a trifle red; he translated it as measles. In those conditions, our job would be too easy. You're merely suffering, my young friend, from a slight alimentary intoxication. Twenty-four hours of fasting and take a nice walk…"

Will my arrival on planet Celia provoke the premature death of my double? My father, summoned, has total confidence in Dr. Hagiotte's science. My mother expresses doubts. Finally, they go in search of another doctor, who diagnoses measles. "There's no mistaking it!"

This success brings me back into the good graces of the family, which Maxime had ill-disposed in my regard without specifying the reasons for his hostility. For fear of contagion, Lucie is sent to stay with a neighbor.

I keep my double company. He has looked up his disease in a medical dictionary and dreads complications. The pause is beneficial to him. All three of us are there. My mother admires my courage and devotion. I listen to Maxime's projects. His self-confidence is so solid that he begins to trust me again. He gives me letters to send to Fanny. They make thick packets.

"You must think me very stupid," he remarks.

"No—I was young once myself."

I know that Fanny will not reply. She's about to depart for a long voyage. She has asked to see me again sometime, as a friend, when she has "a heavy heart." Maxime, she has told me, "is a thing of the past."

Receiving no reply, he becomes agitated. "She's gone away," I tell him.

"How do you know?"

"She wrote me a brief note."

"Show me the letter."

"I didn't attach any importance to it. I tore it up."

"Where is she?"

"In England, I think."

"With whom?"

"I don't know. As soon as she comes back, she'll let you know."

He pretends to go to sleep.

My mother comes in. I put a finger on my lips and go out on tiptoe.

"You don't think he's getting worse?"

"He'll be able to get up the day after tomorrow."

"He seems so low…"

"Sentimental reasons."

"I don't want to be indiscreet…"

"Don't worry."

"It's so frightening: a son who's getting away from you. He hasn't fallen under the influence of a bad woman, at least?"

"No."

"You're sure of that?"

"I give you my word. He's fallen under the influence of a woman who no longer wants him."

"Is that possible? And should I be pleased?"

"Certainly."

"Love," my mother murmurs. "What a terrible thing!"

"Undoubtedly—but in this case, it's not a matter of love."

"Don't abandon him. Watch over him. His father has no influence on him."

That short illness was for me, formerly, a return to the sensibility of childhood. I await the first emergence.

The countryside…an excursion to Saint-Germain in a charabanc, led by the father of one of Lucie's friends. Lucie is there, with her friend, Cécile. An idyll is sketched out between Maxime, who has been gripped by a desire for purity and has made good resolutions, and that pretty girl, who seems to me to be intelligent and wise. The return is effected by night.

"What imprudence!" cries my mother. Wrapped up in cloaks and blankets, Maxime is the object of the most tender attentions. Cécile has surreptitiously taken his hands, which she warms in her own…

When we get back, my father, who is waiting for us, remonstrates with his wife and me. "Danger!" he warns us. "First of all, one does not marry at Maxime's age."

"Why not?"

"And secondly, do you know why these people have a charabanc? Because they use it, during the week, to deliver cream cheese. He's a dairyman.

"Wholesale!" objects my mother.

"Wholesale or retail, he's a dairyman just the same. I don't know what would become of Maxime without us. He sows his wild oats and amuses himself—so much the better. But to marry a dairyman's daughter! He'd be the first member of the family to suffer such a misalliance…"

I consult Lucie. She shares the paternal opinion. There will be no further question of Cécile. While convalescing, Maxime has had a moment of weakness. Cured, and more valiant than ever, he will resume the course of his exploits. Nothing can prevent him from becoming what I became…

I would abandon him gladly, if it were not for my mother…

XII.

The servant of my uncle and godfather indicates that I should join the queue of inquirers in the waiting-room. I ask him if he has received precise orders to this effect. He replies affirmatively and tries to block my way. I elbow him to one side. He cries out. I slip a *louis* into his hand. He shuts up. And I go onto the medieval study where Félix-Amédée Portereau is shuffling papers or banknotes in the depths of a drawer. He closes the drawer precipitately and cries out: "No one can come in when I'm doing my accounts! I shall sack my manservant."

"I'll take him into my service. He'll have no regrets."

"He's a mental defective!"

"All the same, he might have some good stories to tell."

"Bravo, Monsieur! You're a master-singer. They're right to say: like father, like son. Get out!"

"Don't try to play fast and loose with me. I know your game. There's no longer any deception between us. You're trying to play me along and profit from the ideas I can give you without paying me a centime..."

"Have you a signed paper?"

"I have very god papers, with which I could have you locked up."

"Really. Under what pretext, I pray?"

"I have ten of them...a hundred..." I had none—but one risks nothing in threatening a rogue of that sort. "I think that Camille Portereau might claim some enlightenment on the subject of certain inheritances from which you have profited, the Devil knows why…"

"Monsieur, I have one foot in the grave…"

"The other is excellent."

"Heart disease…"

"You can no more have heart disease than a beggar can die of indigestion from eating truffles. Have no fear!"

"Would you take 30,000 francs as a once-and-for-all settlement?"

"I want my due. I've chosen you to take care of my business…"

"So I'll be your agent, after a fashion?"

"Yes."

"Very funny."

"And as you've been busy—I know your faults, but I also know your qualities, and you've already been at work….come on, old chap…"

"I'll thank you to show respect!"

"You haven't a face that inspires respect."

"He insults me! Be careful!"

"Unpack the depths of your sack."

"What annoys me," he said, adopting a softer tone, "is that if I were to give you lots of money, you'd use it to the advantage of Camille Portereau. I have my sources. The daughter has you in the palm of her hand: a schemer! And the son ought to call you out…"

"That's none of your business. You're capable of hatred, then?"

"I don't hate anyone."

"Good. That makes me feel a little more kindly disposed toward you. Hatred is a human emotion; I thought you incapable of it."

"What do you take me for?"

"I took you for a commercial ledger, duly pagi-nated, will well-aligned figures. Get out your files, and quickly!"

"Let's address one another informally," conceded Félix-Amédée, meekly, "since we're family. But there you are, getting worked up—positively flying into a temper. It's permissible I suppose, to discuss things. Out off all your nonsense, I've retained the ladies' nail-varnish. It's ugly, but it's new. We'll get it manufac-tured—it will distract me. Oh! The little paper sheaths for toothpicks—it won't bring in much, but it's practica-ble enough. Since you want to become my partner, you'll have to contribute to the expenses. By the way, I've found that receipt. You owe me 700 francs. That's something to remember—I'm in no hurry."

All the same, he enters that unexpected cash deposit in his books avidly. He gives me a speech about the sa-tisfaction I ought to feel on paying off a paternal debt. "You can't stop there, though. The other creditors aren't interested parties…"

I leave prudently. I dread that a roof-tile, adroitly dislodged by Félix-Amédée, might fall on my head. I'm not afraid of dying, but I have a double mission to ful-fill—firstly for the general well-being, to inform these poor people what lies ahead of them; and to save my family…

Several means of action: the pen, oratory. I'm no longer very certain of my eloquence. In any case, ha-ven't I risked too much to obtain, after so many proofs, the seat of a contemplative *député*? People would be all the less inclined to listen to me if I had important things to say, and I'd soon be classed among the eccentrics. I'd run into the realists. A realist is a man who lives from day to day, acquainting himself, for his own advantage, with current facts: a summary method, but a practical one. I already know that it's a bad idea to be scornful of microscopic events that seem enormous in the light of the present. The masses have no taste for eternal things, and the enormous majority of minds is quotidian.

A brochure: *A Prophetic View of the Future*, signed X? Prophets go unread...

A lecture?

I settle for the lecture. I choose a hall, whose manager shows me round.

"You can seat 350 people here. It's understood that your lecture shouldn't have any political slant. I know all about that: one proceeds very calmly, more for amusement than anything else, and then the debate heats up; fanatics break the chairs and I reap the consequences. Have you chosen a title?"

"Yes: 'What will tomorrow bring?'"

"Tomorrow? But people are fed up with tomorrow! You might get away with it, I suppose, with a few interludes. A little dance? I can recommend an exceptional dancer...no? A pianist who can make more noise than a great orchestra all by herself? A 500 franc fee, negotiable. Or a child prodigy who recites fables, plays the violin and draws caricatures of famous people? No? Just you, and that's all!"

"I'd like to invite the press."

"We can invite them, but I can't guarantee that they'll come in droves. We'll charge a franc for the seats You can't expect to make a profit, but you'll get publicity."

"If you wish."

I drafted a press release. I tried to excite curiosity by promising sensational revelations.

Only one newspaper has mentioned my release. It has inserted it under the rubric of "For a little amusement..." I didn't know that such abuses of humor were contrived in 1896.

My lecture will last an hour, but the public will have value for money...

I am about to talk to the crowd. It's 3 p.m. The lecture was advertised for 2:30 p.m. The audience is composed as follows: seven paying customers who are taking refuge from the rain, as they might in a doorway; in the rows reserved for the press, one adolescent, who has taken out a notebook and is visibly whetting his irony.

Mother is there, with Lucie. In the gallery, one sole silhouette: that of Choute. I have plucked her out of poverty; she now has a genteel mercer's shop. She is extremely grateful to me.

It doesn't matter. The words that I dispense today will bear their fruit.

They did not come in large numbers, but they laughed a lot. The paying customers did not regret their outlay. My prophetic insights into the future stunned the at first, then cheered the up, then made them laugh. Finally, they decided to interrupt.

"I predict for 1914 a bloody European conflagration," I had proclaimed.

"Don't worry about that," shouted a fat gentleman with a jovial and ferocious face. "You won't be mobilizable any longer!"

"And you," I reply, "will be selling rotten conserves to the soldiers."

"Eh? Come on, now, be polite!" ripostes the fat man, taking offense. "If you know me, I don't know you..."

Mama struggles as best she can with interjections. "Shh! Let the lecturer speak." Choute, bellicose, heaps insults upon my adversaries.

I notice that Maxime, having arrived late, is applauding me, but is not the last to laugh...

I have been speaking for a quarter of an hour. I stop and conclude: "You're only a very small group. That isn't important: great things have had equally modest beginnings—but I hoped that a restricted audience would be capable, if not of understanding me, at least of listening to me. I appear to most of you to be the worst of imbeciles..."

"Yes," voices affirm.

"You're cretins!" Choute proclaims.

"Please moderate your expressions, Mademoiselle," declares the hall manager, anxious for his seats.

I intervene. "So, I am the worst of imbeciles—but I have had the text of the lecture, of which you have only heard a third, printed; it will be distributed complete. Keep it—and later, you will observe, hopefully with some remorse, that the stupidity, on this occasion, was not on the stage..."

"Wait for me under the elm-tree!" exclaims the fat man. "When I think that I paid 20 *sous* to listen to this nonsense!"

"You will be reimbursed."

The manager hands me a little note at the exit. There were seven paying customers, but he has paid me for eight seats. The mystery is impenetrable.

Only Mama comes to console me. "Don't take any notice of them," she advises. "They're not worth the trouble."

Choute kisses me. She's crying. She's humiliated on my behalf. "Maxime," she says, "didn't show much courage. In his place, I would have fought. He made me a sign asking to wait for him. I'm going to give him a piece of my mind."

An article has appeared, which represents me as a hideous old man who has realized a fortune by means of various crooked enterprises. Félix-Amédée has written to me rebuke me. "Mind your own business."

Lucie: "You've paid Pioulette 3000 francs for a canvas with a violet tree, red horses and a green sky. Perhaps you have the best intentions in the world, but you're encouraging him. He's persevering in that vein, which is rendering my marriage impossible, for I can't tolerate people making fun of me. Mind your own business."

And that makes two!

There's more. After leaving the lecture, Maxime interrogated Choute. He asked her what she was doing there. She replied hotly. I'm her benefactor. Thanks to me, she has opened a little shop, which has liberated her and permit her to think about something other than suicide. He found her feverish and vehement, reproaching him for the neutrality of his attitude. And Maxime, upset by Fanny's departure, has recovered a sudden interest in the girl who flung harsh truths in his face.

He has just written to me. He doesn't want to know the reasons that incited me to support and save Choute, but he suspects that I have abused the situation. He enjoins me to seek my adventures outside of his own relationships in future. He does not want to bring up my more-than-suspect attitude with respect to Fanny, but he knows from a reliable source that she has run away to escape his persecutions. Finally, be asks me to mind my own business. And that makes three!

Monsieur Levacourt has asked to see me. He wants to get rid of Fougeix. "He's so vulgar that he sickens people, and does us a great deal of harm. You're like me: you believe in elegance. One example: we have recently buried a poet who was not devoid of a certain talent. He was called Verlaine. He never amounted to anything. I saw him once: he dressed like a carter, wore a greasy felt hat and a tramp's muffler. Forgeix is the Verlaine of the drapery business, minus the talent. Then again, he gives up at the first sign of trouble. I put him on the track of some business…a lollipop, my friend; he only has to bend down and pick it up. A customs dodge. He's there. He quibbles—thanks to him, it's all come unstuck. What does the filthy swine need to live? Ten thouand francs a year. You come in on the scheme, and we'll pay him back. I'll roll my sleeves up and put my shoulder to the wheel…"

"I'm not getting involved in the scheme."

"Why not?"

"Not me and—understand this clearly—no one in my family."

"I can see that you're I a bad mood."

"Especially not Camille Portereau."

"Who mentioned that imbecile?"

"Take note that I'm serious, and not talking idly."

"And I'm advising you to mind your own business!"

And that's four!

And five, for he has alerted Forgeix. The latter has just rolled his paunch all the way to my apartment. He doesn't want excuses, but explanations.

"It appears," he tells me, "that you've offered Levacourt a considerable sum to take my place, just as we were about to make a big killing. Look at me, my dear Monsieur. Do I look as if I were born yesterday? You've brought back habits from your pampas that won't wash here. You have your sources? I have mine. I didn't make my money in the white slave trade, like you and your father. Ah! Ah! That surprises you! I say to myself: 'But where does this fellow's insolence come from?' It's a small world and everything comes out in the end. It's only mountains that don't run into one another. I have an old friend who knew Monsieur Raymond Portereau very well. That doesn't worry you?"

"Not in the least."

"You have a strong stomach!"

"And you're what they call a rotten egg."

"Always the predictions. With regard to which I congratulate you on your triumph."

I interrupt him. "Is this a declaration of war, Forgeix?"

"I'll begin by sacking your cousin."

"I strongly recommend it, in his own interest."

"He might die of starvation."

"Don't worry—I'll look after him."

Forgeix looks at me as my godfather looked at me when I threatened to take on his manservant. He hesitates. "I'll make him choose between you and us…if you

150

continue to interfere. But even though I don't look it, I'm a diplomat; I have finesse. I'd rather leave here with a nice peace treaty…"

"Than a kick up the backside?"

"Than a kick up the backside," he approves, ingenuously. "I'm not afraid of you, of course. The best proof is that I'm thirsty. Pour me a glass of whatever you like, as long as it's not water. I don't want to risk being poisoned, do I?"

He emits a belly-laugh. His anger has dissipated. It has been vanquished by thirst.

"You'll let Camille Portereau alone, Forgeix?"

"If, in exchange, you'll mind your own business. Ah, the brigand! He has stout—that's my favorite tipple…"

And six. A message from Mama: "Camille has something urgent to communicate to you. He will expect you at the house today, at 7 p.m. I hope that you can dine with us."

My father has asked to see me alone, in the drawing-room, behind a side-table that might pass for an office desk—the place where he stood to scold me when I hadn't worked hard enough at school. Freshly tinted, my father's beard and hair are black. In a week, they'll be chestnut, in three weeks, almost blond; in a month his blond will go grey. He offers me a seat, and he gets straight to the point, with the violence of the timid.

"You will be kind enough," he tells me, "to mind your own business. Thanks to your ridiculous intervention, I'm just received a ticking off from Messieurs Forgeix and Levacourt such as I haven't received since I started working for the business—which is to say, since

1866. They've told me to choose: them or you. I've chosen."

"Do you know where they're taking you?"

"Yes, Monsieur—to retirement."

"No, to something terrible."

"Don't say another word; I would have the regret of no longer hearing you. And know this: that if Messieurs Forgeix and Levacourt ask for my signature tomorrow on a blank sheet of paper, I will give it to them. If they ask me to sell the little that I possess I will sell..."

"And if they demand your honor?"

"I will give it to them. It could not be in better hands. There is something that is bigger than all of us: the business. I've lived for it; I'm ready to die for it. Monsieur Forgeix has not concealed from me that you have the intention of offering me an advantageous situation. I refuse it. I deem that I am attached to those gentlemen like a pilot to his wheel—like a pilot, not a mussel on its rock. You heap gifts upon us, but as my son remarked to me yesterday: 'We haven't asked him for anything!' We lived before you, we shall live without you—excuse me for telling you that so bluntly."

"You are excused everything. Just write down this date—and later, when it is too late, you will think: 'My God, if I had only listened!'"

My mother opens the door.

"Our cousin," my father pronounces, emphatically, "cannot dine with us. Tell him that you regret..."

My mother says nothing. She guesses that I am being sent away—and for the first time, she feels pulled toward me: an impulse of her entire body, as when I was very small and was about to fall...

"Don't forget," she says to my father, "that André is a member of our family."

My father remains impassive.

I hear Maxime come in quietly and barricade himself heroically in his room…

XIII.

The only person who has uncovered a mystery in me is Fanny. On the evening of our last meeting, I watched her sleeping. Some creatures devoted to an animal existence recover a sort of purity in sleep. By instinctive coquetry, she smiled. A tulle-veiled nightlight painted pink make-up over her face and throat. I thought: *I once mistook her for a monster, but she's only a poor child.* Suddenly, her smile vanished; she uttered a faint moan and opened her eyes.

"Go back to sleep," I say.

She sits up, passes her hands over her forehead and mutters: "My darling, who are you?"

"Who am I?"

"Yes, who are you?" Without waiting for my reply, she adds: "I beg your pardon, that's absurd—but you scare me. I can't explain you. You're good, my darling, and I sleep so sweetly in your arms. You even know everything that I'd love to hear, and which no one has ever said to me. I know more about you than most of my lovers, and yet you scare me, but make me afraid to cry. It seems that there's something you're not telling me— something frightful. I'm telling you everything, you see. Tell me—you can trust me. Tell me..."

"Oh! Well..."

For two pins, I'd confess to this girl, as murderers do. She would cry: "Madman!" She would run away in her night-dress...

"Very well! Go find some champagne. You're rambling; you need to pull yourself together."

She gets up quickly, as if to flee from a phantom, and runs off to fetch a bottle and two glasses. The curtains are open. She's surprised. "It's not daylight yet…"

As she drinks, he glass breaks between her teeth. I give her mine, full, which she empties in a single draught. "Ah!" she sights. "That's better. What came over me just then? A vision! I asked you who you were…as if I didn't know. Only you're never coming back—I'm sure of that. You look at me, and you look at me, as if from the depths of sadness. I need to go abroad, with a friend, It's better for me to go, isn't it? In the interests of my gaiety…"

Animals that like me also scent a mystery in me that humans, save for Fanny, don't suspect. Dogs come to me, but if I bend down to stroke them, they run away. Some of them welcome me with a strange ululation, and their masters murmur: "What's got into him?"

When I got old, I kept a few photographs from my youth. I looked at them sometimes. Between those mute conversations and those that I have had with my double there is scarcely any difference. And what he has been able to say to me is worth less than all that I learned from those portraits…

I've received these lines from Lucie: *Dear cousin and great friend, I need to ask you for some advice, but it's impossible to talk with an open heart in those family evenings when one only emerges from banalities to enter into disputes. Unless I hear to the contrary from you, I'll come to your apartment at 10 p.m. tomorrow. Don't mention this to a living soul, and believe that I'm your friend.*

Again, Lucie misunderstands me. She must have thought many times about the item of jewelry that I offered her, and which she refused. The idea of a marriage with a rich old gentleman was repellent to her then. She has got used to it...

At my home, she offers herself—modestly, of course, but she does offer herself. I try to send her back to Pioulette. She shrugs her shoulders...

I shall not prevent Pioulette from leaving alone and despairing, from renouncing his art in order to try to make money. He will die of fever, fatigue and disgust, in some sinister hovel, in the company of an opium-addicted colonist and an indigenous servant. The portrait of Lucie that he has painted, with his genius and love, will realize 250,000 francs at public auction in 1931. Pioulette will, in spite of everything, bring money to his beloved.

A bittersweet remark from Lucie by way of a Parthian shot: "Well, I wasn't misinformed. I can see that you aren't too bored in Paris!" She closes the door a little too forcefully...

I have disappointed her. She hoped to become a bride, and announce the news to her ironic and curious comrades: "My cousin is no longer very young, but he is still so seductive! And he's so clever, so generous..."

Of all my teachers, Monsieur Mizonnex was the only one who ever took an interest in me. I wait for him at the school gate. I see him, hunched up in his worn overcoat, his hands gloved in wool, his hat pulled down over his white hair. I intercept him.

"I'm a relative of Maxime Portereau..."

"His father? I'm pleased to meet you..."

"No, a cousin. He's often mentioned you to me."

"What, he still remembers me?"

"Yes, gratefully."

"I wasn't able to do much for him. What has become of him?"

"Business…"

"He wasn't entirely an imbecile…"

"I'm delighted to hear you say so. I'm interested in him…"

"Pupils that rise above the general stupidity are so rare! That one had the soul of a poet, but the instincts of a chamber-pot merchant…"

He laughs, delighted with his joke, and adds: "In such cases, it's always the chamber-pot merchant that wins. I'm glad to have met you, Monsieur."

And he turns away, in a hurry to get to his obscure literary works, misunderstood by everyone, which would hopefully render his name immortal 30 years hence…

XIV.

Throughout my peregrinations I have kept the winged ball that will permit me to correspond one last time with the Earth. I put the ball in a suitcase and I go to the Bois...just as I followed Varvouste on a similar night. My excuse is that I can't undertake an excursion into my Past. I want to leave...

Some words from Horace come back to me: "Is it sufficient to flee to escape oneself?"[19] At the end of this adventure I have only encountered one thing: myself. I have been able to pass judgment on my youth. With a little reflection, it would have been unnecessary to go so far.

The weather is very arm. Couple in love pass by in open carriages.

The ball contains a summary of my adventures and a few scientific observations made during my voyage through space. I entreat Varvouste to take the capital that I left at his disposal in a bank, to construct an apparatus as quickly as possible. If he cannot come to look for me himself, he may hire, with means I shall furnish, a benevolent explorer—but he will come. I shall expect him. I give him various directions: he must take every precaution to ensure that the apparatus does not blow up when it touches down. I give him my address. I have not omitted anything.

_____

[19] I have translated the protagonist's version of this sentiment directly rather than rendering the quote in its usual English form ("What fugitive from his homeland can also escape himself?")

I pay the coachman and set off into the Bois. My hands are trembling. I have learned Varvouste's instructions by heart.

The key…

The ball does not take off—but two men emerge from a thicket. "What are you doing?"

"As you can see, I'm playing with a balloon."

"All alone?"

"All alone."

"A singular distraction for a man of your age. Show it to us."

At that moment the ball, whose mechanism I have re-set, trembles between my fingers and lights up weakly. The policemen, who think I am in the process of preparing an anarchist outrage, run away precipitately. I have had enough, and I make myself scarce.

Perhaps I shall return a septuagenarian, but I shall return. Yes, one only lives by curiosity, and I want to know what is happening on Earth…

I cannot win any glory here by predicting the future. At the most, people will say: "Well, that's odd! That man wasn't mistaken. Mere coincidence!" And the coincidences are accumulating, without my inspiring more confidence. The world of 1896 was not accessible to the marvelous. But my return with Varvouste, with good evidence in my pockets…

I'm going to leave.

I'm sure that Varvouste has set to work. A few months to construct the apparatus…I shall wait. As my imagination is sharp, I believe that departure is imminent, and I recover my indulgence for everything that I am going to leave behind…

Presentiment confirmed. A newspaper announces, in three lines, the appearance in the sky of a singular meteorite. Several Japanese and American astronomers have been able to make observations: the meteor was of a previously unknown form.

I'm certain that Varvouste has followed me, and that his arrival is imminent.

Choute, pursued by Maxime, has found no better means of getting rid of him than telling him that she was my mistress. It appears that he is looking for me...

"Be careful," Choute warned me. "He's half mad, and he detests you."

It's in a public place that Maxime has run into me. A fair held in the Tuileries one afternoon. He advanced towards me with his can held high. I don't remember having made that gesture before. I have, after all, upset the established order of things.

"You're absolutely determined to fight?"

"You're a coward!"

"You've already said that. Well, so be it—let's fight. I await your seconds. I hope that you'll arrange things so that your mother knows nothing about it."

"Mind your own business!"

But where can I find two seconds? No need to search far: my concierge and the manservant that my godfather will lend me for the occasion. My godfather accepts. "Your concierge and my ruffian! I'll make myself a pint of good blood! You must be adept with a sword. Don't kill the simpleton, but give him a good lesson."

I've received Maxime's seconds: Gomieux and Lehors, a nice chap of whom I retain no memory—a specialist in affairs of honor. For such solemnities he wears a funereal uniform, somewhat faded but impressive. "Would you care," he says to me, "to put us in touch with your seconds?"

"Just one word…"

"You have only to communicate it to the gentlemen to whom you are sending us."

"You are familiar with the rules in matters of dueling, as am I. They specify that a debtor cannot, under any pretext, square up against his creditor."

"Agreed."

"Has Monsieur Maxime Portereau not informed you that he is indebted to me for a certain sum?"

"No."

"If you would care to pay it on his behalf, I can provide this affair with the sequel it requires."

"We shall," the technician stammers, "refer this to our friend. It must be an oversight on his part."

"An oversight that he will be incapable of repairing."

"Probably," Gomieux confesses.

"Well," I said, "we're worthy fellows. This conversation will remain confidential. We shall make a promise."

"Word of honor," specified the technician.

"Here's the 4000 francs. I'll put in 500 francs for various expenses: doctor, location of weapons, the landau and the traditional breakfast. To put Maxime's conscience at ease, you can tell him that you were able to procure this sum…"

"Implausible!" Gomieux remarks.

"So be it! Take him the receipt with the 25 *louis* supplement. He won't ask for details."

Lehors stands up straight. "Monsieur," he says to me, "you're a gentleman. Maxime is also a gentleman. It would heartbreaking to see two gentlemen cutting one another's throat over a girl. Maxime is young; he takes everything too seriously. As I've told him: 'At your age, one is never deceived; one deceives oneself, and one gets over it!' I think we may be able to draft a legal statement, that we can place in the newspapers: *In consequence of a material error, honest explanations have been exchanged, etc.*—and the incident will be closed."

"We have received a formal mandate," Gomieux explains. "Maxime will not be content with a legal statement. He will insult you in public."

"In that case," Lehors decides, "the duel seems indispensable. At any rate, have no fear, Monsieur. I shall supervise the combat, and I shall make sure that it concludes with a scratch and a reconciliation."

I shall rely on the reconciliation, especially, and make sure that it is me who is scratched.

Meudon wood. My seconds are not very sparkling. The concierge has only one thought: to keep away from any pistol. He has seen in numerous humorous drawings that bullets sometimes hit the wrong target. Lehors arranges everything with great dignity. He murmurs to me *en passant*: "How you resemble him, though! We must all breakfast together."

And here is Maxime. He throws out his chest, but he deems that Choute is causing him a considerable annoyance. He must have—as I always had in such circumstances—a dry throat and a tongue stuck to his palate…

"Go, Messieurs!"

I had thought he was going to throw himself into my arms, but he is throwing himself upon me, with the evident intention of killing me once and for all. His fury is divided between Choute the origin of the conflict, and me. I am too self-controlled, very formal. I break and, with a curt thrust, I disarm my adversary: myself!

The doctor I have brought passes the fallen weapon through a solution of phenol.

"It's better like that," the concierge remarks. "The doctor has sterilized the swords."

I intend to be wounded, slightly—not too much, for my task is not finished. Ten times I have an opportunity to touch Maxime, but that is not my intention. He gets excited, tries to get too close, and the technician has to intervene with his cane.

Finally, at the seventh reprise, I obtain what I'm looking for.

"Halt!" cries Lehors.

A drop of blood pearls on my wrist.

"I haven't hurt you?" Maxime enquires.

"No…imbecile."

"Ah!" says Lehors, smiling. "No insults. We aren't going to start again. Embrace!"

Maxime embraces me.

"Your mother knows nothing?"

"No, nothing."

The doctor applies a light bandange.

"Shall we eat together?" Gomieux proposes. He points to my seconds. "These gentlemen won't find it inconvenient, I suppose."

"Unfortunately," I say, "their affairs recall them to Paris. Thank you, my dear friends. I shall see you soon."

A faint cry. It's Choute, doubtless warned by Maxime. She has witnessed the duel. She emerge from a faint. We comfort her. Maxime takes her by one arm, I by the other—and she squeezes my arm with a vigor in which there is remorse. She turns back to Maxime, who has, after all, just fought a duel for her. She will continue to serve him as a distraction during the intervals between his sentimental adventures. There too, I have failed…

Lehors is a combative drunk, Gomieux a tearful one. Lehors settles the bill with a part of my 25 *louis*. I feign a protest.

"Please!" cries Maxime.

But Lehors makes a grand gesture. "It's necessary that you know: Monsieur has been marvelous. He's the one who wanted you to represent yourself on the field free of any obligation—for you had neglected that small detail. Thanks to you, we nearly passed for bumpkins. If you don't know the Code of Honor, I'll teach you."

"I'm at your disposal!" says Maxime. "You don't imagine that you frighten me?"

"Firstly, I always thought it disgusting that you challenged a man of that age. I keep quiet while I'm a second, but afterwards, no one can prevent me from speaking."

"Yes—me!" howls Maxime.

"Oh, no!" begs Choute. "You're not going to spend your whole life fighting!"

I appease Lehors. I calm Maxime down. And, piled into one of the landaus, we go along the Allée des Acacias. On seeing us, the passers-by search the second landau in vain for the bride of which the second landau is devoid.

"Come to the house with me," Maxime said. "It's necessary to clear up all the misunderstandings."

They are waiting for us, Maxime having told everything to his sister, swearing her to secrecy, and Lucie having talked. I find my mother on the point of fainting, between her husband and her daughter. My father is pale.

"Finally!" cried my mother. André, it isn't possible—you wanted to kill my son?"

"A duel!" says my father, supportively. "That's a fine thing! And you claim that we are cousins. A duel between two members of the family. It's unprecedented!"

"A simple joke that I arranged," I say.

"It's very clever, and I congratulate you both," snaps my father. "I had to ask the gentlemen for an afternoon's leave, and Rose is sick with anxiety."

"What happened?" asked Lucie.

"Why, nothing."

"Nothing," Maxime adds. "But I wounded him, all the same."

"It's frightful!" my mother groans. "Have you at least been well cared-for, with no consequences to dread?"

"All is for the best, since we are all together again. Let's not mention it again."

"I've alerted Alexandre," my sister says. "In case he comes, I'd be grateful to you to spare him your encouragements. I've obtained a promise that he'll become serious."

"Likewise with Messieurs Forgeix and Levacourt," says my father. "Be good enough not to intervene with them in regard to me. There's a possibility of promotion. The slightest stupidity might muddy the waters."

In sum, they are all asking me to let them follow the sad course of their destiny.

"I understand. I wanted to see you one more time before leaving…"

"Where are you going?" asks my mother.

"Perhaps you'll find out one day, and will be astonished. I'm going away…"

"I think," decides my father, "that it will be as well. You're no longer accustomed to our country. I understand that. I had a friend who spent several years among savages. He stifled in Paris. I will shake your hand, André. With no hard feelings, *bon voyage*—and write to us occasionally…"

"But you must come back." My mother begs.

"I'll try. I'm not sure."

"At any rate, it's goodbye," declares my father, lightly. "I shake your hand affectionately, my friend."

"Keep this," I say. "If, in three months time, you have heard no word of me, this letter authorizes you to enter my apartment. This key opens a little box. The number of the combination is 303. You'll find an envelope with five red seals, on which I've written: *For Rose*…"

I give the key to my mother, who stands there nonplussed.

"And you'll be able to take care of many things…if the need arises…"

Maxime thanks me. I am convinced that my father will subsequently issue orders that the key should be thrown away and that no one should give me a further thought. That is how I interpret the long look that he directs at me, charged with suspicion.

"Come on," he instructs Maxime. "I expect that you've wasted enough time."

In the envelope there is all the money I could raise, plus a hundred thousand francs that Félix-Amédée has given me, having desired to see me sign a receipt "in full settlement" before the encounter. "I know full well that these duels are farces, but one never knows what might happen."

Lucie is intrigued, but the maid comes in to announce Pioulette. She prefers to receive him in the dining-room, without my presence.

"Rose…"

"André?"

"We shall never see one another again."

"But if…"

"Promise me that you will respect what I call my last wish."

"This envelope?"

"It's yours."

"I don't know if we can…"

"I love you very much, Rose. I'd like to spare you…"

"A misfortune?"

"Anxieties… Watch over your husband. Make him promise that he will never confront you with a *fait accompli*, something irreparable…"

"You're frightening me…"

"And all will be well."

"I don't know what you mean, but I'm sure that you mean well."

"Would you do something for me?"

"Certainly."

"I'm about to leave you. I'd like to hear you say to me…don't laugh…it's rather bizarre…you might be my daughter…"

"Go on. What would you like to hear me say?"

"Once—only once: 'Goodbye, my dear son.'"

My mother smiles, touched by this fantasy. "Gladly, André."

"You don't need to understand?"

"You once had a mother who adored you…"

I kneel down. She takes my head in her slender hands, which are trembling slightly. "Goodbye, my dear son."

"Goodbye, Mama."

The staircase with its fake marble. I climbed it slowly; I go down more slowly still. Never before, between my mother and me, was there an effusion as tender as the one I have just extracted from myself. Never, even after the catastrophe, when I saw her suddenly grow old, the mainspring of her life—honor, not that of fuels but that of a name—having been broken. Never. A kind of modesty…

Three more lines in the newspapers. The appearance of the meteorite has been observed in San Francisco, Yokohama, the Hague and Vienna.

Varvouste will soon arrive in Kahlenberg.

I shall go to Kahlenberg. We must not waste a minute on this retrograde planet. I shall demand that Varvouste take me back immediately. I need electricity, central heating, the wireless telegraph, my automobile and my contemporaries—even those I despise the most. Perhaps I shall have a few more years of tranquility, in the glory. After the most insignificant life, the apotheosis…and what an apotheosis!

I am sufficiently softened. The egotism of yesteryear comes back to me like a cold blast.

I await Varvouste as I once awaited a desired mistress: I imagined her face and evoked her voice, her first words. It was a torturous sweetness, which made me wish, secretly, that the wait might be prolonged…

It seems to me that I see him glide down, and land.

I hear myself: "Quickly! Let's go! What happens here is not of the slightest interest. I'll tell you all about it, but first, bring me up to date."

The return...

I also heard the hubbub of the ovation: "Hurrah for Varvouste! Hurrah for Varvouste!"

And a faint voice: "Goodbye, my dear son..."

My maid is frightened.

"Monsieur, while you were away, policemen came."

"What did they want?"

"I don't know. They fired questions at me. Then they searched everywhere."

"What for?"

"A machine, so they claimed. I told them that they were mistaken, that Monsieur is no anarchist—quite the contrary, seeing that he is rich and his opinions are everything they ought to be. They took away Monsieur's lecture."

"Nothing else?"

"Nothing else."

"Did they say that they would come back?"

"No, but they might. When those people get an idea in their heads! They asked me Monsieur's profession. I replied that Monsieur had the air, primarily, of being an inventor, and that he probably writes in verse. Monsieur must excuse me, but Monsieur has not told me anything much, so I did my best."

They will come back. They will ask for my identity papers... "Here, Thérèse, here's some money. My affairs require me to go away..."

At night, I dig up the ball that the policemen were unable to find. I pack my suitcase in haste. I'm ready.

Either they'll abandon the trail, or they'll send me a letter summoning me to the commissariat...

At 3 a.m., I make a tour. The house isn't being watched. Let's take advantage of that...

I walk for two hours. I hail a cab and have myself taken to the Faubourg Montmartre, in front of the Cité Bergère. I leave the cab, go through the Cité Bergère and come out into the Rue Rougement. From there, another cab takes me to the Gare de l'Est.

XV.

Vienna.

And Kahlenberg.

There are still traces of conflagration at the place where I came down.

I take a room at a nearby inn, and only go out after dark, in order not to encounter any of those who picked me up and cared for me. I tell the innkeeper that my eyes are painful and that daylight makes me feel ill. The man is so loquacious that, only being able to jabber a few words of French, he finds the means to extrapolate those few words into interminable conversations. He is eager to please and often employs a "Me too!" that he thinks flattering: "My eyes are hurting." "Me too." "Here are you're your cigarettes." "Thank you." "Me too."

"Meteor in the sky," I say to him. " Phenomenon. Bright light. I saw it."

"Me too."

I push the interrogation as far as I can with the aid of my pocket dictionary. The inhabitants of Kahlenberg thought it was lightning, but it wasn't at all like the lightning-flashes that form zigzags. It was a sort of sparkling streak.

"Magnificent!" the innkeeper judges. And he mimes a little dive, commenting proudly: "Me too!"

I emerge from the inn, the collar of my overcoat turned up.

A young girl goes by. *"Ponchour, M'sieu…"*

I make no reply. I thought I recognized my little nurse—the one who cared for me tenderly when I arrived…

I'm registered under the name of Klenner, resident of Lucerne.

Prudence!

It is three weeks since I emerged miraculously from the flaming apparatus.[20]

I wait, as placid and sure of myself as a Parisian waiting for a bus.

By the light of a dim lantern I am writing these final notes in pencil. The night is splendid. The return will be a pleasant voyage. I am determined only to take the drink and food that is strictly necessary. Unfortunately, the night is rather chilly, and a painful rheumatism has almost paralyzed my arm…

The fourth night. The stars are hidden. I can see two men advancing in the distance…two men to my left…two men to my right…

Have I been spotted? It's not certain. But why are they encircling me?

Suddenly, I recognize one of the hideous male nurses who put me under the shower…

Perhaps they only want administrative explanations. In any case, I need to send this story to Earth. I activate the little machine, which lights up…

I must stop here.

---

[20] This statement is blatantly inconsistent with the time-scheme of the story, which includes an earlier assertion that the protagonist was in the lunatic asylum for an entire month; readers must make up their own minds as to whether the inconsistency is deliberate or not, or what it signifies if it is deliberate.

XVI.

This manuscript was found in a field near Mantes-Gassicourt, in Seine-et-Oise, by an agricultural worker who extracted it from a bizarre machine, cylindrical in form, which was three-quarters buried. Technicians have examined the little apparatus but have been unable to establish with certainty its construction or its origin. No trace has been found of Maxime-Félix Portereau or the inventor Varvouste. Perhaps the real names have been modified, but in the opinion of all reasonable people, it can only be a hoax or the work of a madman. A small margin remains for the Impossible. Men of science agree that certain aspects of the machine present curious particularities that are presently inexplicable.

The paper of the manuscript bears an 1896 watermark.

Finally, it was possible to decipher the following lines, traced in pencil and partly washed away by rain, on a ragged piece of paper:

I shall kill myself. It's no tragedy: it was always my destiny to be good for nothing. Farewell, all those I loved so badly. The time has come for the voyage from which no one ever sends back news, doubtless out of disdain. Come on, Maxime, you need to go...better that than find yourself again!

SF & FANTASY

Guy d'Armen. *Doc Ardan: The City of Gold and Lepers*
G.-J. Arnaud. *The Ice Company*
Aloysius Bertrand. *Gaspard de la Nuit*
Félix Bodin. *The Novel of the Future*
André Caroff. *The Terror of Madame Atomos*
Didier de Chousy. *Ignis*
C. I. Defontenay. *Star (Psi Cassiopeia)*
Charles Derennes. *The People of the Pole*
Harry Dickson. *The Heir of Dracula*
 Sâr Dubnotal *vs. Jack the Ripper*
Alexandre Dumas. *The Return of Lord Ruthven*
J.-C. Dunyach. *The Night Orchid. The Thieves of Silence*
Henri Duvernois. *The Man Who Found Himself*
Win Scott Eckert. *Crossovers* (non-fiction; 2 vols.)
Paul Féval. *Anne of the Isles. Knightshade. Revenants. Vampire City. The Vampire Countess. The Wandering Jew's Daughter*
Paul Féval, *fils. Felifax, the Tiger-Man*
Arnould Galopin. *Doctor Omega*
V. Hugo, Foucher & Meurice. *The Hunchback of Notre-Dame*
O. Joncquel & Theo Varlet. *The Martian Epic*
Jean de La Hire. *Enter the Nyctalope. The Nyctalope on Mars. The Nyctalope vs. Lucifer*
G. Le Faure & H. de Graffigny. *The Extraordinary Adventures of a Russian Scientist Across the Solar System* (2 vols.)
Gustave Le Rouge. *The Vampires of Mars*
Jules Lermina. *Mysteryville. Panic in Paris. To-Ho and the Gold Destroyers*
Jean-Marc & Randy Lofficier. *Edgar Allan Poe on Mars. The Katrina Protocol. Pacifica. Robonocchio. Tales of the Shadowmen* (anthos.; 6 vols.) *Shadowmen* (non-fiction; 2 vols.)
Xavier Mauméjean. *The League of Heroes*
Marie Nizet. *Captain Vampire*
C. Nodier, Beraud & Toussaint-Merle. *Frankenstein*
Henri de Parville. *An Inhabitant of the Planet Mars*

Polidori, C. Nodier, E. Scribe. *Lord Ruthven the Vampire*
P.-A. Ponson du Terrail. *The Vampire and the Devil's Son*
Maurice Renard. *Doctor Lerne. A Man Among the Microbes.
The Blue Peril. The Doctored Man. The Master of Light*
Albert Robida. *The Clock of the Centuries. The Adventures of
Saturnin Farandoul*
J.-H. Rosny Aîné. *The Navigators of Space. The World of the
Variants. The Mysterious Force. Vamireh*
Brian Stableford. *The Shadow of Frankenstein. Frankenstein
and the Vampire Countess. The New Faust at the Tragicomi-
que. Sherlock Holmes & The Vampires of Eternity. The Stones
of Camelot. The Wayward Muse.* (anthologist) *The Germans
on Venus. News from the Moon*
Kurt Steiner. *Ortog*
Villiers de l'Isle-Adam. *The Scaffold. The Vampire Soul*
Philippe Ward. *Artahe*

MYSTERIES & THRILLERS

M. Allain & P. Souvestre. *The Daughter of Fantômas*
Anicet-Bourgeois, Lucien Dabril. *Rocambole*
A. Bisson & G. Livet. *Nick Carter vs. Fantômas*
V. Darlay & H. de Gorsse. *Lupin vs. Holmes: The Stage Play*
Paul Féval. *Gentlemen of the Night. John Devil. The Black
Coats: The Companions of the Treasure. Heart of Steel. The
Invisible Weapon. The Parisian Jungle. 'Salem Street*
Emile Gaboriau. *Monsieur Lecoq*
Steve Leadley. *Sherlock Holmes: The Circle of Blood*
Maurice Leblanc. *Arsène Lupin: The Blonde Phantom. The
Hollow Needle*
Gaston Leroux. *Chéri-Bibi. The Phantom of the Opera. Roule-
tabille & the Mystery of the Yellow Room*
William Patrick Maynard. *The Terror of Fu Manchu*
Frank J. Morlock. *Sherlock Holmes: The Grand Horizontals*
P. de Wattyne & Y. Walter. *Sherlock Holmes vs. Fantômas*
David White. *Fantômas in America*

SCREENPLAYS

Mike Baron. *The Iron Triangle*
Emma Bull & Will Shetterly. *Nightspeeder. War for the Oaks*
Gerry Conway & Roy Thomas. *Doc Dynamo*
Steve Englehart. *Majorca*
James Hudnall. *The Devastator*
Jean-Marc & Randy Lofficier. *Royal Flush*
J.-M. & R. Lofficier & Marc Agapit. *Despair*
Andrew Paquette. *Peripheral Vision*
R. Thomas, J. Hendler & L. Sprague de Camp. *Rivers of Time*

CINEMA

Stephen R. Bissette. *Blur 1-5* (non-fiction) *Green Mountain Cinema 1* (non-fiction)

HEXAGON COMICS

Franco Frescura & Luciano Bernasconi. *Wampus 1*
Franco Frescura & Giorgio Trevisan. *CLASH*
 Luciano Bernasconi, Jean-Marc Lofficier & Juan Roncagliolo Berger. *Phenix 1*
Claude Legrand, Jean-Marc Lofficier & Luciano Bernasconi. *Kabur 1*
Franco Oneta. *Zembla 1*
Lina Buffolente, Jean-Marc Lofficier & Jean-Jacques Dzialowski. *Stangers 1: Homicron*
Danilo Grossi. *Strangers 2: Jaydee*
Claude Legrand & Luciano Bernasconi. *Strangers 3: Starlock*

ART BOOKS

Jean-Pierre Normand. *Science Fiction Illustrations*
Raven Okeefe. *Raven's L'il Critters*
Randy Lofficier & Raven OKeefe. *If Your Possum Go Daylight...*
Daniele Serra. *Illusions*